Dangerously In Love

By

Jordan Silver

Copyright© 2014 Alison Jordan

All Rights Reserved

Table of Contents

Chapter 1

ROMAN

Hi I'm Roman Blair I'm a twenty-year old college student. My girl Vicki's in her last year of high school, she and I have been going strong for a year and a half or so, ever since we first met.

I met her one day while out and about in our small hometown of Goldlake Oregon. Let's just say she captivated me from the start. I saw her from afar and was hooked. Something about her just screamed 'that's all you bro'.

So I became her stalker, well not exactly but it was close, wherever Vicki was, I was sure to be. If she was going to be at the local diner hanging out with friends I would find myself in a booth not too far from theirs. If she and some of the girls were going into Northwick I was right behind them.

How did I know so much about Vicki's goings and comings? Easy. Vicki and my little sister Petra were BFFs or whatever the hell girls were calling themselves these days. Anyhow it was summer break and I was hot on Vicki's trail, I clocked her every move before I finally made mine. She gave me a run for my money but in the end that shit was no match for a Blair male on the hunt.

Needless to say I won the girl, now the only fly in my ointment was Timothy Crafton, Vicki's supposed childhood friend. I hated that fucking guy from day one. He was way too territorial when it came to my girl. Like the first time she introduced us and he kept crowding her, talking about shit that I had no idea about to keep me out of the conversation. My girl wasn't down with that shit though, so she made sure I was included. That's the only reason that douche still had all his molars.

We dated heavily for three months before my girl let me make love to her completely. My baby was a virgin, she wasn't about to give it up to just anyone and I respected that. Besides she was only sixteen and a half at the time and I was nineteen. Before you cry statutory rape, the age of consent here is sixteen. I'm not that kind of guy. Besides she knew she was on lockdown from the get. I'd let her know in no uncertain terms that she now belonged to me. So whether I took her virginity now or later it was all good. The shit was mine.

Obviously this isn't about how we met and fell in love we're way past that, this is about where we're at after the kiss. Let me explain.

Something happened about six months ago. Vicki and I broke up for two months. Here's how it happened, Vicki got all twisted out of shape about this crazy chick named Megan. Megan and I met at a party. I of course had no interest, but this chick was obsessed or some shit. She started following me all around campus, somehow getting ahold of my number and texting or calling at all hours. I tried to put her off without hurting her feelings too much but nothing worked.

Of course as these things go she texted me some X rated shit one weekend when I was home from school. It was one of those long holiday weekends, and since I was addicted to my girl I made sure to be home as often as possible. Being away from her was fucking torture, but dad said I had to stick to my Ivy League school that was a million miles away.

Needless to say I got my girl setup with some Apple products, so we could do FaceTime, Skype, whatever it took so we could be together. It was hard but we managed. We'd committed to each other.

Now back to the infamous text, since Vicki and I had no secrets from each other she and I were in and out of each other's phones all the time. Then that Fatal Attraction bitch fucked my shit up. Needless to say Vicki was not amused to hear how much throat action Miss. Bennett could give a certain appendage on my anatomy. No matter what I said she wouldn't believe me, she convinced herself that I was away at school fucking anything in a skirt. So she broke up with me, almost fucking killed me.

Apparently while we were on our hiatus the douche saw this as his opportunity to move in on my territory. What he didn't understand and what I knew wholeheartedly was Vicki and I are meant to be. It was one of those love of a lifetime things with us. Although it was killing me to be apart from her, I still kept tabs on her through Petra, who was only too happy to help her brother out. She's a romantic at heart.

So while I'm giving my girl time to cool the fuck down and get her head out of her ass, this piece of shit decides to move in on my shit. Lucky for him she rebuffed him or I would've thrown his ass off a cliff.

By the time summer break rolled around again she had come to her fucking senses and we were back on track. Now a little less than six months later this shit happens. What happened?

I'll tell you. I was on my way to my girl and happened to see her old beat up truck parked outside Goldlake diner. It was winter break and I was home a few days early.

When I pulled into the parking lot she was coming out, but she was not alone. That fuckwad was there. I couldn't make out what he was saying to her but it was obvious they were arguing. I was about to get out and go to her when that asshole put his hands on her. I saw fucking red, but what really did it is when the red haze cleared and I was halfway out of my car; she was kissing him back. How do

I know? She had her fucking arms around his neck.

I couldn't think of anything else to do but blow the horn. When she realized it was me she looked like her life was about to end. Me, I just stared at her in disbelief. I don't think I had any feeling in my body for a good two minutes. And what was that fucking douche doing? He was smirking at me, the fuck.

Chapter 2

ROMAN

Needless to say after that debacle I burned rubber out of the lot with Vicki running behind my car. I couldn't even look at her right now. How the fuck could she? I seriously had to pull over and puke my guts out on the side of the road.

Now I'm the first to admit I'm not the most rational of human beings and I don't forgive worth a fuck. What this meant for us was anybody's guess. Right now I couldn't think worth shit; my mind was in a haze and I think my heart had stopped because I couldn't feel it. There was a ringing in my ears and I wanted to pass the fuck out. I barely made it to my family's estate without crashing out.

Vicki caught up with me at the end of my driveway. I slammed on the brakes and jumped out to confront her. I didn't want to take this shit to my house where my whole family was sure to be in attendance. Too many fucking questions.

"GET!THE FUCK!OUT OF HERE." I was fucking seething.

"Roman it's not what you think." She backed away from my anger her face red from crying.

"Not what I think, it's not about thinking Vicki, it's what the fuck I saw. You disgust me stay the fuck away from me and my family. Go fuck your friend for all I care." I spat at her, literally in her fucking face. That's how fucking mad I was, me, Roman Blair, the guy who opened doors and pulled out chairs.

I turned and headed back to my car. I didn't give a fuck about her tears or her pleadings. I drove away hoping she heeded my warning because if she followed me I was afraid of what I'd do. I wouldn't be able to control my anger for much longer.

For the first time in my life I wanted to hit a fucking woman. I seriously wanted to slap the fuck out of her then go find that asshole and gut that fucking dog. Now I know you're probably wondering 'well why didn't you fuck them both up then and there?' That's easy, couldn't think straight for shit. That shit shocked my system or some fuck. If you knew what this girl meant to me you'd understand but I can't even put that shit into words. Seeing that shit literally pierced my fucking heart, so right about now I'm a wounded fucking animal. A wounded animal doesn't fight he heals first and then comes back for the motherfucker he's marked for death. Besides it was her ass I hated at the moment, I give a fuck about him.

I slammed through the door, not stopping to greet anyone. I heard my mom calling for me but I ignored her and kept going. I didn't want to talk to anyone, I was so fucking mad I thought I might do serious harm to the next person to get in my face.

I'd changed my whole fucking life around for her and she did this shit to me. I was on the fast track to becoming a doctor before I was twenty-two. Yeah I forgot to mention I'm some kind of prodigy, the only reason I wasn't a doctor as yet was because I wanted to become a specialist. That obviously takes more time. Fuck I care.

I could've done my residency at any one of the major hospitals in the country, but in order to be close to her while she finished her schooling I'd chosen the local hospital.

They were only too happy to have me. The grant monies they'd receive because of my tenure there would keep them up and running for a long time to come. Everything was perfect. I had our lives all mapped out and was doing everything I could to make sure she stayed happy.

Now this shit! How the fuck am I going to stay in the same town as her now? Fucking sap.

I really fell for her act too. All innocent and sweet, I wonder how long she'd been fucking him behind my back? Don't think about that shit or you'll really fucking lose it. I tried to shut it down, to get away from the buzzing in my head and the fucking pain in my heart. I refuse to fucking cry and I fought every instinct to go on the hunt. I'd always thought that if I saw another man touching what's mine I'd kill him dead. The thing is I'm not mad at him I'm fucking pissed at her though.

Vicki must've texted and called me fifty times in the last half hour. I deleted the text and ignored all her fucking calls. As far as I'm concerned she could go fuck herself.

I had my iPod in my ears listening to some hardcore rap, which usually soothed me, and I needed some major motherfucking soothing right about now.

Petra barged into my room unannounced.

"What the fuck Petra?"

"Roman you're being stupid." My little pixie of a sister did not seem too happy. I was sure her pal had called her and given her version of events, too bad she was full of fucking shit.

"What the fuck are you talking about?" As if I didn't fucking know.

"You know Vicki would never do what you're thinking."

"Get the fuck out of my room. Some sister you are."

"Roman listen to me before you throw away the best thing that's ever happened to you."

"What the fuck is there to say? I saw them with my own two eyes, the best thing that's ever happened to me apparently is a two bit skanky whore."

"She was only trying to prove a point Roman."

"Yeah, what point is that, that she's a two timing slut? They've probably been laughing at me behind my back all this fucking time." I knew talking about this shit was going to make me feel violent. Petra needed to back the fuck off before she got the backlash.

"Oh Roman, she made a stupid mistake, her heart was in the right place, she just used poor judgment that's all." She was starting to cry, and though I usually couldn't stand to see the women in my life cry, I couldn't find it in me to give two fucks. Shit...I wanted to mother-fucking cry.

"Why don't you take some time to calm down and then let her explain?"

"Get the fuck out. NOW Petra. " She huffed out of the room. Was she mental, did she not know me at all? I saw what I saw. No amount of talking was going to change that. Shit I didn't want to know why the fuck she did it, there's no fucking excuse.

I hate a fucking cheat.

Chapter 3

ROMAN

For two whole weeks I stayed away. I went to Portland to spend some time with friends and just try to chill the fuck out. There might've been some drinking involved so the fuck what, who gives a shit?

I turned off my phone my second day there. Between whoriana and my sis that shit kept ringing off the hook. I don't know why the fuck they couldn't leave me in peace, couldn't they understand I was done?

I'm not the guy you do that shit to, not, at, all. Just saying.

The weekend I returned home one of my boys was having a party. I usually didn't have much interest in that shit but what the hell! I'm a free agent I can do what the fuck I want. The real reason I stayed away from these things was because of Vicki. She wasn't allowed at parties where there was going to be booze and drinking. With her father being the sheriff she tended to be a stickler for the rules, so out of respect for her I steered clear as well. Too bad she wasn't a stickler for other things.

The party was in full swing when I finally arrived. There were half naked bodies everywhere. Couples were hooked up in every available corner, some were getting hot and heavy on the couch.

I saw Petra for a fleeting moment but thought nothing of it. Her and Damien had been circling each other for the past few months so there was no surprise at seeing her here.

That annoying ass Tiffany Sawyer was here as well. Between her and Megan I don't know who was worst. She'd been stalking my ass for two fucking years; even when I was with Vicki she'd been relentless.

I said hi to a few people but didn't stay in one place for too long. I headed out back to grab another beer with Tiffany trailing behind me with her annoying ass voice grating on my nerves. She kind of cornered me. I was about to blast her until I saw Vicki standing in the doorway. Without giving much thought to what I was doing I grabbed Tiffany and kissed the fuck outta her. That shit was nasty as hell and it left me cold.

I heard Vicki gasp my name and felt a moment of guilt before I squelched that shit. I was a free agent; she made that choice when she let that fucker put his hands on her.

Tiffany heard her and turned to her with a smug smile on her face. Okay honestly, that shit pissed me the fuck off. Vicki turned to flee her shoulders slumped. I saw the glistening of tears in her eyes and felt like shit.

Why the fuck should I feel guilty? We weren't together anymore, when she did that shit we were in a committed relationship, where was her guilt then?

"I never knew what you saw in her mousy ass anyway. I'm way more woman than she'll ever be." Tiffany piped in."

I was about to school her rancid ass but since she said that shit loud enough for the mouse in question to hear I never got the chance.

Vicki turned around and punched the fuck outta Tiffany knocking her out cold. Get the fuck out. Layla Fucking Ali.

Chapter 4

ROMAN

Obviously things got a little hectic after the title round bout. I needed to wake the screeching owl and Vicki was looking like she'd had an outer body experience. It was my natural inclination to go to her and comfort her, but nah, wasn't happening. I clearly saw the irony in the situation though.

By this time a crowd was gathering so I sat Tiffany up and got her back on her feet. She was a bit groggy not knowing where she was at first, but I was sure it'll come to her eventually. I'll wait and see what play she was going to make. As much as I detested my ex I didn't want anyone else fucking with her.

Surprisingly she didn't make too much of a stink, just a few choice words for Vicki, a threat here and there and then she flounced out when she realized the kiss was just a one off and I wasn't harboring any deep seated love for her.

I bailed after that, having lost all interest. I didn't want to be where she was, still too soon. She made moves like she wanted to say something but I rebuffed her. I'm sure all who hadn't known that we were over before that night now knew.

The holidays were here, two days away. It was supposed to be a joyous occasion and I was gonna do my best to make it so. Mom had me running around doing errands, which was fine by me since I needed to keep myself busy. Less time to think.

I had a fuck load of presents I had bought for little Lolita before she fucked me over. They were gonna stay in the bottom of my closet collecting dust, I couldn't bring myself to give them to anyone else. Besides you don't just throw around Tiffany's and Cartier, especially when you put a lot of thought into it for a specific person.

On my way back from one of my many errands I happened to pass the infamous diner. I had avoided this place like the plague for the last couple of weeks and believe me. That's not so easy to do in a small town.

I don't know what the fuck made me look but I did. I saw her beat up piece of shit truck parked outside, and wonder of wonders the dog's bike was there.

Something inside me snapped, my vision blurred and my head swam. I was out of my car before I knew what the fuck I was doing. I entered the diner, looking around for her. She was sitting at a booth in the back, luckily for her she wasn't touching that motherfucker.

I walked over to her, not even acknowledging his ass. I pulled her out of the seat before she even knew I was there.

"Hey." The asshole started to get out of his seat.

"Don't even think about it fucker." If he wanted to jump off I was all for it. I've been taking Krav Maga since I was twelve I would fuck a motherfucker up, seriously. He got away once not this time, this time my anger was a little more contained, which meant I was more of a danger to both their asses.

"Timothy it's okay." She held her hand up placating him while I dragged her out of there.

"Don't fucking talk to him."

There were a few bystanders who looked interested but I didn't pay them any mind. I wish I knew what the fuck I was doing, I just knew seeing her with him was not an option.

I threw her into my car and headed home. I saw the douche in the rearview watching us leave. I wanted to give him the finger, but he didn't matter. She sat there not saying anything, just biting her nails nervously. I didn't say anything either my blood was too hot right now.

I took her inside holding her upper arm in such a way that she was walking lop sided, she knew better than to protest. I had a feeling I was scaring the shit out of her but couldn't bring myself to care. I'd given her gentle and gentle got me fucked.

I marched up to my room. Mom could wait for the shit she had me pick up. Pulling her into my room, I cornered her against the wall, both hands on either side of her head.

"What were you doing with him?"

"We were just talking." She looked nervous as hell.

"What the fuck do you have to talk to him about?"

"Roman we're just friends."

"Do you let all your friends shove their tongues down your throat?"

"It wasn't like that."

"Yeah? Well then, tell me how it was I'm listening." Why am I doing this shit to myself? Because you're in love with her you sap and you're hurt and pissed and confused and what the fuck.

I have an enlightened brain but this shit still brought me to my fucking knees. There's no escaping emotions no matter how fucking smart you are.

"I was trying to prove a point, I know now that I was stupid but at the time it seemed to make sense."

"The point Victoria-Lynn."

"I wanted to prove to him that I didn't love him, that I love you. I thought if I kissed him and he saw that it meant nothing then he would ease up on the whole two of us getting together thing."

"And if I hadn't seen you, would you have told me about the kiss?" She squirmed like a fish on a hook.

"Thought so. So by your reasoning, I should shove my dick down Megan's throat, you know just to prove to her that I don't want her sucking my dick. Or better yet Tiffany, she's been trying to suck my dick for the longest time.

What do you think Vicki, does that work for you?"

She was sobbing and hyperventilating, see how it feels bitch?

"If I ever see you near him again, I'm going to fuck him up so bad not even his father will know him, and then I'll deal with your ass."

"You don't want me..."

"You fucking kissed him in the middle of the fucking parking lot of the diner for everyone to see. Everyone in our little town who knew you were with me, how fucking stupid are you?"

"Please don't yell at me, I said I was sorry." She covered her ears.

"You're unfucking believable you know that. You had a fucking melt down from a text, a meaningless text from a thousand fucking miles away, but you think I should just forgive you for betraying me."

"I didn't betray you, please Roman, please." I looked at her for the longest time not saying one fucking word. I still wanted to smash her face, but I wanted to kiss her more. I did neither.

"You want another shot, you're gonna have to regain my trust and things are not going to be the same as before."

She started nodding before I was through speaking. I hope she knows what she's getting into I have a lot of pent up anger to assuage.

Chapter 5

ROMAN

I fucked her six ways from Sunday, up against the wall, bent over a chair. I dragged her onto the floor and pounded out my anger in her. I bit and sucked every visible part of her body while I was at it. Let her explain that shit to the sheriff, this way that fucking dog and all the other motherfuckers in this town will see my mark and know who owns her. She took it all like a champ and gave as good as she got but I still wasn't done with her. She hadn't learned her lesson yet.

"You have to earn my bed again." I whispered that shit in her ear when I was finished pounding her into my bedroom floor. It was cruel. A dick fuck thing to do and it made her cry, but what the fuck? By fucking her I'd resealed the bond that should be good enough for her for now. Did she think I was a pussy to just roll over and take that shit? Hell fucking no, don't let the Gucci suit fool you, I'm a hard motherfucker when I wanna be. I forgive, eventually, but I never forget, that's for motherfucking chumps.

"Get cleaned up and go home, go straight home Victoria-Lynn, no stops, no phone calls and no text with Timmy Boy. Tomorrow we're going into Northwick and getting you a new phone with a new number." She was on a plan with the sheriff, she could fucking explain to him why that was no longer needed I didn't give a fuck. I'd already bought her the iPad and the Mac Book, why not the fucking iPhone too. Now she'll be on my plan and there would be no reason for him to have her new number. Some might say that's too over the top. Fuck, You. You weren't in that fucking parking lot getting your heart ripped the fuck out. I'll do me thank you very much and you can do you.

She walked the best she could into my en-suite to take a shower. There were still some of her bath products lying around in there. It's a wonder I hadn't gotten around to tossing that shit; in fact I'd been too fucking mad to think of shit like that. I still had all our pictures, though the one from my nightstand was in the bottom of the drawer with a broken frame.

She came out of the bathroom freshly showered, head down biting her lip. I was sitting on the edge of my bed watching her.

"Come here Victoria-Lynn."

She came over to me quiet as a lamb. I stood her between my knees and looked in her eyes for the longest time.

I kissed her hard then soft, nibbling on her lips while feeling up her delectable ass. None of that was for her though that was all for me. I'd missed the fuck out of her ass.

"I'll have Petra take you back to your truck."

I saw the hurt that caused. I was treating her like a fuck, not like the love of my life. Before I would cuddle her after making love. Sometimes I'd even bathe her, pamper her and cherish her. Sheeeiiit, we were a long motherfucking way from those days. She got the dick, now she had to earn my heart.

I heard her explanation. It was all bullshit to me, whether she meant to prove a point or not, she let another man touch what's rightfully mine. Now I have a point to prove. No, Fucking, Way.

"Remember what I said, no contact whatsoever. If you're walking down the street and you see him get off the fucking street, walk somewhere else. If he says Hi, you become a dumb, deaf and blind mute. In other words Victoria-Lynn, if you ever acknowledge his existence again We, Are, Through and I fucking mean that shit." She started to say some shit, maybe that he had been her friend for a long time or some shit which had been her argument in the past. Not this time fuck that shit. He gave up that card when she had to prove a point to him, maybe this time he'll fucking get it. She never finished whatever the fuck she was going to say. Good she was learning already.

She nodded her head, tears running again. I wiped them away. What! I'm not an animal. I kissed her forehead, patted her ass and took her downstairs to find Petra. Sis was only too happy to see us back together, I could see the questions churning behind her eyes but she didn't say anything. Mom who knew something had been up but not quite what was warm and welcoming, she always liked my girl.

"Vicki, sweetheart it's so good to see you. What are you and Kenneth doing for the holidays?"

"Dad's working, uhm, I 'll be home I guess." She looked down kind of embarrassed.

Mom looked at me to say something, maybe to invite her to eat with us, I kept my mouth shut, let her sweat. Petra was shooting daggers at me with her eyes, like I cared. Mom had the good sense to drop it. It was my decision after all.

I didn't even wait around for her to leave, just turned and headed back upstairs. Don't think it wasn't fucking with me to treat her this way. It was, but she had fucked up almost beyond repair; short of knocking the fuck out of her, which I'm pretty sure I could never do, this was the next best thing. I tried to think of what it would be like if I just walked away. I'd given that shit a lot of thought in the past few weeks. But each time I did my whole fucking body revolted. She was in me somehow, a part of me. There was no letting go fuck that.

Chapter 6

ROMAN

The next day I picked her up to go shopping. She was wearing a turtleneck and skinny jeans under this kick ass bomber jacket I had ordered her from Italy. I really wanted to see under that damn sweater to see my marks all over her. If I had my way she would be wearing a tank top or some shit, so everyone could see how I'd marked what's mine, but I guess it was too cold out for that shit. In the car the tension was heavy and that shit was getting on my nerves. Why the fuck was she sulking?

"If this is gonna work you're gonna have to stop that shit."

"What?" She looked at me like the innocent girl I once thought she was.

Yeah I'm still bitter, so, the fuck, what?

"That sulking shit, don't act like I did some shit to you, this is all you. And before you open your mouth to say shit to me, I don't want to hear it. Tomorrow's Xmas I want to salvage whatever joy I can out of the season seeing as you fucking destroyed it already.

Damn I really am fucking pissed. I've never talked to her like this before, but somehow I can't seem to stop, every time I open my mouth I just feel this need to hurt her.

I checked her out out of the side of my eye. She looked like she wanted to fucking cry. I felt bad, sorta, but I needed her to get how fucking serious I was about this shit. This fuck was never to be repeated ever again in life.

Usually on a drive like this we would be laughing and touching, always touching. I miss her fucking hand in mine. We would be fighting

over whose iPod to listen to and shit
like that, but I didn't feel like doing
any of that shit with her. Until she
proved to me that she was the girl I
loved, this was the way things were
going to be.

It was the day before Christmas
and the stores were packed. We headed
straight for the apple store where I
chose her phone. Then I took her to
this other place that mom and Petra go
to to get their phones dressed the fuck
up.

She liked this diamond and pink
sapphire case with hearts and roses on
it. I dropped a grand and a half for it
and we were done. Money isn't the
objective with us, it doesn't matter how
much or how little I spend on her, it's
all of me she wants. I'm holding back
the best part of me for now and she
knows it. Too fucking bad, she could
deal or not the choice was hers. For her
sake I hope she can deal otherwise
she'd better make plans to move,
because there was no way she was

going to live in our town and be with another motherfucker, no way no how.

"Let's have a coffee." I led her to a coffee shop and sat her at a table while I went to order, a coffee for me, and one of those froufrou things she likes with a crap load of milk.

When I came back there was a douche trying to talk to her, she looked scared out of her fucking mind. Now I don't want my girl to be some timid mouse, afraid of me and shit and I sure as fuck wouldn't hold her responsible for shit she has no control over. The girl is absolutely gorgeous so obviously motherfuckers are gonna try. It's my job to send their asses packing, but not for her to be afraid of me, I'm not down with that shit.

"Dude, be gone." I didn't even look at him, but he left without a peep.

"Roman I..."

"Vicki don't be stupid, you damn well know I'm not gonna get mad at you because some guy tries to hit on you, it's not the first time and it won't be the last. You know damn well what this is about." Motherfucker, aren't you the one who said you didn't want to talk about this shit? I wish my subconscious would shut the fuck up.

"Change of topic, let me see your phone."

I took her phone and programmed it for her, setting up all the bells and whistles. When I was through with it I would be able to find her in a cornfield in full bloom.

Was I the kind of fucker who would check up on her? Damn straight, until my guts untied from the sailor knots that they've been in the past few weeks, and I get the picture of that fucker's' hands on her out of my fucking head you bet your ass.

I don't know how many points she might think she has to prove. A bit much huh, I, Don't, Give A FUCK. Being cheated on is no walk in the park, and yes it's cheating. Even if she'd just held hands with him in that way couples do it would be cheating in my book. We belonged to each other, her body was mine and mine belonged to her that's all the fuck there is to it.

She's lucky I kissed her yesterday after she kissed that fucking mutt. If I were a real asshole I would've made her gargle first.

"How long are you going to be mad at me?" That sweet angelic voice damn. I wanted to tell her all was forgiven and just go back to the way things were, but this shit was too important to me, this lesson had to be learned.

"I thought I told you we're not discussing this shit the day before Christmas? Now drink your froufrou shit, your phone's set." She took it from me and checked it out. Her face was lit up like a kid in a candy store, my girl do like her gadgets.

"Thank you Roman." She gave me a quick tentative kiss on the cheek like she was afraid I was gonna rebuff her. I grabbed her and pulled her into my lap and kissed the shit out of her. That just lead to thoughts of other things and all of a sudden I was in a hurry to head back.

"Let's go." I took her hand and headed out.

Chapter 7

Victoria-Lynn

Roman's really mad at me, I've never seen him this mad before, he's always so laid back and happy. This is really killing me cause I didn't really mean anything by the stupid kiss. I was just trying to prove to Timothy that there was no spark between us, not like there is between Roman and I. But of course Timothy had to take it too far and Roman had to see that.

I can't imagine how he felt watching that, I know I hated seeing him kiss Tiffany Sawyer. I don't think I could ever see her again without wanting to do bodily harm and if Roman felt that way, then Timothy was in serious trouble.

Tomorrow's Christmas and it looks like I'll be doing it alone, not that that would be anything new. It's just that last year I'd had Roman and his family. Our relationship had still been new, but they had welcomed me with open arms.

When Natalia asked me about dinner and Roman didn't forward an invite I wanted to die, but at least he was talking to me again.

The sex had been out of this world amazing, not the soft tender touches I was accustomed to, and I missed that but it was still hot. I hope though that we could get back to the romance, he wouldn't even make love to me on his bed, that hurt.

This morning he came to pick me up to go get my new phone. Kenneth hadn't made too much of a stink when I'd told him about the changes. He knew Roman and I were joined at the hip at least we used to be. He didn't know anything about our split though, thank goodness.

Now we're speeding back from Northwick after getting the phone and there's a different kind of tension in the air. I knew what this meant. When we first started making love we could hardly keep our hands to ourselves. It didn't matter where we were, Roman would take me down and mount me. There've even been times when he'd sneak through my bedroom window in the middle of the night with Kenneth sleeping down the hall. It didn't matter to us we couldn't get enough. Now he would hardly hold my hand. How could one stupid mistake cause so much damage?

ROMAN

I barely brought the car to a stop inside the garage before I was on her.

"Take these off." I pulled at the zipper on her jeans. I was rampant I needed to get inside her like I needed my next breath. I pulled her turtle neck down and bit and sucked on her neck while she peeled out of her jeans in the confines of my Aston. This was going to be a tight fit. As soon as the jeans were gone I pulled her over my lap, tore off her thong, released my dick and brought her down on me. She cried out at the force of my upward surge.

I grabbed her hips in a too tight grip and pushed and pulled her on and off my length all the while mouth fucking her.

"Take your top off I wanna see my tits. She obeyed without question. She was so fucking wet that shit was dripping on my seat. Who gives a fuck? Her tight pussy felt so good on my aching dick nothing else mattered.

I damn near mauled her tits, licking and sucking and biting for all I was worth. She was making these sexy sounds that spurred me on to madness.

"Mine, mine, mine, mine." I pounded up into her so hard her whole body shook but still it wasn't enough. I opened my door and eased us out while still trying to keep her on my dick.

At the side of the car I pulled out, bent her over the hood and slammed back into her from behind. She arched her back and cried out. Thank fuck my family was gone last minute shopping and won't be back for a while, she was making way too much noise.

I grabbed her hair roughly in one hand while choking her from behind with the other.

"If you ever let another motherfucker put his hands on you again I'll fucking end you. You hear me? Answer me Vicki." I punctuated each word with a forceful thrust.

"Ye...yeah." She was fighting for breath. I pulled my hand back and slapped her on her ass with as much force as I could muster. She protested, but I felt a gush of warmth cover my dick. My little innocent baby liked it rough did she?

I spanked her ass a good ten times and no love taps either, these were open palm stingers meant to inflict pain not pleasure. She got the pleasure from my dick, the pain was a reminder that she fucked up. I was a long way from forgiving that shit. Fuck, You.

Chapter 8

ROMAN

I pulled out and ate her pussy from behind until she was juicing all over my face. Then I turned her around and did it all over again. When she started trying to pull my hair out at the roots I knew she was ready to fuck but I had something for her. "Beg me to fuck you." I had my hand wrapped tightly around her throat as I looked into her eyes. I squeezed until she was damn near ready to pass out. "Please…fuck me…" I rubbed my cock up and down her pussy feeding her just the tip before pulling out again. I turned her roughly and bent her over. "I'm going to fuck your ass hard. Take it." I eased my cock in five inches and pulled back giving her more and more of my ten inches each time I went in. When she'd taken all of me and was on her toes trying to ease the pressure of having my in her belly I pulled out and slammed back in. She screamed hard and long, her nails dragging across my car.

I grabbed both her arms and held them behind her back with one hand while paddling her sweet ass with the other. "I own you, every fucking inch don't you ever forget that shit again." I bit into her jaw, teased her clit and fucked her ass hard.

When I was through fucking her I took her upstairs to get cleaned up. I'm feeling a lot less tense now that I'd shot my heavy load. In the bathroom I ran the shower and finished getting undressed. Vicki was already naked so we just hopped in. I soaped up her hair while she stood there all drained and shit. I could clearly see where I'd marked her yesterday there were black and blue hickeys all over her from her neck to the crease between her pussy and her thighs. There were fresh ones forming from today's little venture. For some reason seeing that shit made me hot.

I rinsed her hair, held her against the shower wall and with water pulsing over us from four separate jets I drove into her. She wrapped herself around me tightly as I worked my pussy for all it was worth.

We kissed for so long and so hard we were in danger of passing out from lack of air. I finally freed her mouth to give her some much-needed air. I'd missed her fucking kiss.

"You love me? " I rocked back and forth into her.

"Yes." She looked me in the eyes when she said that shit, again my dick received that warm gush from her pussy.

"Say it." I strummed her clit with a little more force than normal.

"I love you Roman always." By the time the words were done my tongue was back in her mouth. I slowed my strokes and shifted my angle. I hadn't been giving her any G-spot action lately I figured I'll give her a treat. I hit that shit and she went the fuck off.

My dick bore the brunt of it when she clamped down and squeezed that motherfucker. I wasn't ready to come yet. It's going to take me a while after the garage. I planned on wringing at least five more of those out of her though.

I'd reached that point where I needed more friction so I took us to the bottom of the shower. The marble was nice and smooth so should be no hardship on her skin; the power of my thrust was a whole other story though.

I had her legs over my shoulders leaving her wide open, my dick was happy as it plowed through her like a hot knife through butter. From this angle I was deep, so deep her eyes were crossed, my toes were curled and my balls were drawn tight as a bowstring.

"Come Vicki, I bit down on her nipple and she screamed, cumming in one continuous orgasm that seemed to go on forever.

I pulled out, not even close to cumming yet. I rinsed our bodies quickly, dragging her out the shower and into the bedroom. The bed was looking good as fuck but not yet.

I went over to my lounging chair and sat down pulling her into me with her back against my chest. This way I had easy access to her magnificent tits. I palmed them gently before pinching and pulling her nipples. She rode me hard and deep as I pushed up to meet her downward thrusts. I used her tits to pull her up and down as hard as I could while I attacked her neck with my teeth.

I think I'd reverted back to the fucking cave because all I wanted to do was own her heart body and soul. No kidding, I had this sudden need to own every aspect of her life. I wanted to control her and that shit scared the fuck out of me.

No I didn't want her to be afraid of me, but I wanted to run her, make all her decisions for her, tell her where she could and could not go, who she could and could not see. What the fuck happened to me?

Subconsciously I knew this was a result of that fucking kiss, but I had to ask myself if I hadn't always had that in me.

Whatever the case maybe she was in for it now, by confirming her love for me she had sealed her fate.

Chapter 9

We cleaned up afterwards and I took her home before my family returned. On the way in the car I explained some things to her. Might as well get this shit out in the open. She needed to know that the Roman who loved her and treated her like a fucking queen was still there, but that motherfucker had evolved. The lover was now going to be sole owner and proprietor. Her ass was mine, if she didn't know that shit before she soon will.

"I know what you want from me Vicki, but it's not gonna happen, not yet anyway. Do you remember how you felt when you thought I was cheating on you? Well that was only a thought and it took you two months to even speak to me again. But now the tables are turned only this time you actually did fucking cheat, but you expect me to just say all is forgiven and go on like before. Not fucking possible. First because we're never gonna be the same again and you have to pay for fucking that up. Secondly, it's going to take me a long fucking time to get over what you did and trust your ass again. I warned you before about him, but you swore to me you were just friends. So how did it go from just friends to having to prove a point to him?

I'm not asking you to understand my position, I don't care if you understand, it is what it is. But there's something you should know. You awakened something inside me that was better left asleep, now you have to deal with that shit. As of today I'm taking complete ownership of you. I will curtail your freedom, you won't be able to pick up and go to Northwick without telling me, in fact asking me first. No more hanging with the girls whenever you feel like without me knowing about it. I will tell you when, who, and how. If you can't live with that get out and walk away."

She didn't move an inch, but she did look a little like Bambi caught in the headlights.

Victoria-Lynn

I'm so scared right now, not scared for my life scared, but kinda you know. Only just not in a physical way, I'm afraid that he'll leave me. I was a basket case the last time we broke up I don't think I could survive this time without him.

I didn't understand what he was saying though; he wanted to control me? That sounded like a Lifetime movie of the week waiting to happen. I don't believe for a second that Roman would ever harm me physically, spanking my ass not withstanding, but how far is he gonna go?

I'm not completely stupid, I know most of this is his hurt pride talking. I know my cuddle bear is under there somewhere. My only hope is that when he finally does forgive me we can get back to where we were.

That's the life I'll fight for, that's the reason I'll put up with whatever he dishes out. Because that life was beautiful, it had tremendous promise.

Why couldn't life come with some sort of road map? You know, a GPS that said go here, don't go there do this don't do that. Then maybe it could've warned me what a stupid fuck thing it was to do, kissing Timmy.

Now not only was Roman mad at me but I was losing my best friend. That's another thing, how was I supposed to cut Timothy out of my life completely? We've been friends forever, our dads were practically joined at the hip, and although Timothy had been pushy a lot lately, it was I not him who had instigated that kiss.

I did it to end his nonsense about us trying to be a couple so we could get back to being friends, but look how well that went. I'll have to find a way to keep him away or I could lose the best thing in my life. I could do it his way if it meant getting us back. I just had to work hard to prove to him that he could trust me. Then again I wasn't so good in the proving things department.

ROMAN

I left her at her house and headed back to Northwick. Somewhere between fucking her and laying down the law I had an idea and since it was the day before Christmas I had to move quick.

When I got home my mom and sis went ape shit over my new acquisition.

"Hands off ladies this is for sweet cheeks." I hightailed it upstairs before they could attack the fuck out of me, and set up my new find in my room.

I almost called her but didn't. That's some shit I would've done before, we would spend hours on the fucking phone even if we had just seen each other, it was sweet. I liked sweet I wanted sweet back. Maybe one day I'll get the picture of the two of them outta my head and we'd get back to sweet. Who the fuck knows? Sweet or not, she was mine and she was going to stay mine.

I know that douche is still gonna try to see her, I'm waiting to see what she'll do. If I was worth anything to her! If we were worth anything to her she'd do the right thing.

I spent some time pondering whether to give her her other gifts. I know how much she likes that shit and really it wasn't going to change anything. So in the end I decided to give them to her. You knew you were gonna do that shit anyway. Shut the fuck up you.

Later that night like a fucking sap I headed to her house, okay I missed the fuck out of her alright. Not just the sex, just her, being around her. I missed her laugh, her smile. I haven't heard her laugh in a long fucking time.

I knew the sheriff would be passed out in front of the TV or in bed by now so I climbed through her window. She was asleep on her back the covers half off; her body sprawled all over the damn bed. My girl sleeps wild.

She must've sensed me the way she always does because she opened her eyes and looked right at me. She did one of those stretching while smiling things people do when waking up from a good dream before she remembered that I was crazy boyfriend, then she got just a touch wary. Probably thought I was here to give her another talking to.

I walked over to the bed toeing off my shoes while pulling my shirt over my head. "Move over." She scooted to her side and I climbed in drawing her to me. She smelled fucking amazing and she was wearing one of my old college shirts that she had pilfered before. I loved knowing that she still slept in my shit. That meant I hadn't alienated her with my demands. I still meant that shit though, there's no way I was backing down from that. I needed it. For my own fucking sanity I needed it.

I needed to stamp that fucking dog out of her existence. That's the only way I will be satisfied, when he was no longer a part of her life in any way shape or form. That's the price she had to pay.

Chapter 10

ROMAN

I woke up early the next morning; it's Xmas. I watched my girl's face as she slept, so beautiful, fuck. I'm not surprised that other men like sniffing around her, but where before I laughed that shit off, this experience has taught me I can't be too lax. She has a mile of fucking jet-black hair and eyes the color of the Caribbean Sea. She's short but I like that shit. And her ass, fuck, her ass is a sculptor's wet dream. I studied her as my heart did that happy shit it always does around her. Why baby? Fuck let it go Roman, just let it go for now, just for today.

I know her dad would soon be up and about. Usually by now I would be gone, but I'd prepared well for this. I'd parked a couple streets over no one would mess with my shit I was sure.

I planned on staying until he was gone which should be in about another hour.

I worked my way beneath the covers, pulled her boy shorts to the side and feasted. She woke up cumming in my mouth. She caught her scream in her throat when she realized what was going on. She turned to stone for a second when she put it all together.

We were in her house, the sun was up, her father was home and I was about to fuck her. I guess we'd just have to be as quiet as possible. I pulled her shorts off.

I slid up her body and face planted in her neck as I slipped inside her warm wet heat. Damn she felt good on my dick first thing in the morning. I teased her with slow and easy strokes;

couldn't have the headboard banging against the wall now could we?

I'd barely got ten good strokes in before I heard the sheriff heading down the hallway. She tensed in fear of being caught but I wasn't stopping, the door was locked.

"We're doing this, relax and enjoy." I whispered that shit in her ear as I continued stroking in and out of her. I could tell this shit was exciting her even with her fear because she was drowning my cock with her juices. I went for her breast and had to put my hand over her mouth to muffle her moans. She was pushing up into me silently begging for more so I gave it to her. I hit her G-spot while I bit down on her nipple and she bit the fuck out of my hand as she went off like a rocket.

My dick was loving that shit, she squeezed me so tight I thought she would break my shit off.

"Whose pussy is this Victoria-Lynn?" I growled in her ear.

"Yours, baby." She could barely get the words out they were all breathy and shit.

"Don't you ever forget that shit, it's mine, I'll take it whenever I want, wherever I want yeah!" She could only nod as I took that moment to grind harder into her pussy.

"Vicki you up yet?"

She tried to stop again but I wasn't having that shit I pressed my thumb down on her clit and had her writhing on my dick.

"Tell him no."

"Not yet dad, I think I'm gonna sleep in."

"Good girl." I kissed her ear; her voice hadn't given anything away. I'm sure he couldn't tell I was in there fucking the shit out of her. I kept fucking her while he moved around downstairs.

At some point I threw one of her legs over my shoulder, opening her wider so I could plow deeper into her. Every once in a while I would give her a hard stroke, which shook the bed. I'm not sure if the sheriff could hear that shit or not, I just knew this shit was hot as fuck. It wasn't like at my house, my parents knew we fucked and since I had my own floor it didn't matter what the fuck we did. But this shit was different this shit had danger written all over it.

"Please, please, please."

She was whispering a chant in my ear, but I wasn't ready for this shit to end yet. So I pulled out and worked my way back down her body. I licked and bit her while finger fucking her soaking wet pussy. It's a wonder he couldn't hear that shit through the door. I licked her dry then turned her over, hands holding onto the bed head, while I entered her from behind.

Damn I was so deep in her pussy I was sure I had to be hurting her, but it felt fucking amazing. I played with my sweet cheeks as I fucked her long and hard. Her ass is what got her her nickname; Sweet cheeks, the sweetest ass anywhere.

I guess she forgot her father was in the house or she'd stopped giving a fuck because she pushed back on my cock harder and harder. I fondled her tits and bit into her neck while grinding my cock into her. "Still." She stopped moving, her breathing choppy, her pussy flexing around my cock. I wanted to play. I played with her clit with one hand, pinched her nipple with the other and flexed my cock deep inside her pussy. "Don't move." I bit her ear when she started to move.

"Please." Her voice was a hoarse whisper." I licked down her neck over the marks I'd left there before taking the same bit of flesh between my teeth and sucking hard. I pulled out halfway and slid back in, her body trembled and her hands tightened on the bed. "You sure you want to belong to me?" She nodded her head and turned her mouth for mine. I played with her tongue before sucking it into my mouth. I rode her until she clenched around my cock and it pulsed and spewed inside her. I swallowed her scream as we came together.

After the sheriff left we got cleaned up in their tiny ass bathroom.

"Get dressed lets go." She didn't question me. Good, she always was a quick learner.

She put on a blue cashmere sweater and a pair of skinny jeans with her ballet flats. I knew what all that shit was because my mom had shown it to me when she bought them for Vicki's last birthday. My girl looked hot as fuck.

We walked out the front door and the sight of her truck almost made me see red.

"I'm getting you a new car and you're getting rid of this piece of shit."

"But I like my truck, it has character." She tried to be cute.

"Yeah? Well I'm well aware that that fucking mutt and his old man used to own it and they're the ones who fixed it up for you. There's no fucking way you're riding around in something that he had a part in ever again."

"What will I tell my dad?"

"You're seventeen, you have a boyfriend, a boyfriend who has money. We've been together for more than a year. He'll get over it."

She didn't look too sure but I wasn't backing down, those days were done.

"I can break it to him if you want." Just like I could tell him that in this state at the age of seventeen I could move her the fuck out of his house into mine and I would if he fucked with me.

No way was I asking his permission on the car thing though. I'm well aware her father is team Timmy. Him and the mutt's father were tight, they probably had dreams of their offspring getting together and giving them grand babies. Fuck if I was ever gonna let that shit happen.

The only babies my baby was ever gonna have would come from me. I'd put my life on that. I won't disrespect the sheriff, but he wasn't standing in my way again. I lived with his cold shoulder and snide remarks bullshit to make things easy on my girl but all that shit was dead.

He could accept me or not, his choice, but I'm gonna let him know I'm here to stay. No more of his passive aggressive fuckery. I'm gonna start calling him on all his shit from now on. There's no give left in me. My father always said 'begin as you mean to go on'. Well I'm taking his advice.

"I'm parked around the corner, let's go."

We walked to my car and I drove her to my house.

It was Xmas after all couldn't have my girl spending the day alone. I'm not that fucking heartless.

Chapter 11

ROMAN

When we reached my house mom was the only one up in the kitchen starting preparations for the Xmas spread she made every year.

"Everything went okay last night? " I kissed her in thanks for the favor she'd done me.

"Perfectly fine son, merry Xmas Victoria-Lynn." She kissed her cheeks.

"We'll be right back." I took her hand and led her up to my room. When I opened the door there was a soft whining coming from the corner of the room. Of course she zeroed in on that shit.

"Is that?"

"Merry Xmas baby." She squealed and barely spared me a hug before running to her gift.

I'd gotten her a Pomeranian. I knew how much she'd always wanted one, I didn't see the fascination but what the hell do I know. It looked like a rat with hair to me but she squealed and carried on like I'd given her some extravagant gift.

"Roman are those...tell me these are crystals or zircons."

"Nope."

"Are you insane, you can't put diamonds on a dog, good Lord."

I just shrugged at her, what the hell, the research said that's what the 'It 'people did, so that's what the fuck I did. I 'd gotten the idea from one of her girlie magazines that she'd left lying around here months ago.

I know she was saying that shit but she was secretly thrilled with the pink diamonds. Besides they weren't that big, who the fuck cared?

"Do you like it or not?"

"I love it thank you, how did you know?"

"Vicki you've only been dropping hints about this shit for the last half a year."

"I didn't think you noticed."

"What kinda guy would I be if I didn't notice when my girl was dropping hints all over the place? Put it here." She kissed my lips as I picked her up dog and all, the little shit yipped at me.

"Watch it fur ball before I take you to the pound."

"Roman, don't tell her that you'll scare her." I rolled my eyes. I'd forgotten my girl's quirkiness.

"Sweet cheeks she's a dog I'm not sure she understands what I'm saying."

"Well just in case." She mimed locking her lips.

I kissed her again and put her back down.

"I'm going downstairs, you coming?"

"Can I bring Tinkerbell?"

"That's her name? Geez what kind of froufrou shit name is that for a dog?"

"Uh, she's a girly girl, she has to have a girly name, besides you're the one who bought her diamonds."

"Right, it's my fault you're gonna give the poor dog a complex with that pansy ass name."

"Your daddy's silly."

Damn right I'm the daddy. Shit now I was happy to be the father of a fucking dog. Women made men stupid, I'm convinced.

"Whatever let's go, bring Tinks' carrier if you want or she'll probably tear the place apart. I have all her stuff in the closet to go through later."

"What kinda stuff?"

"Just stuff that every dog needs." Okay so I might've gone overboard with the dog stuff so sue me.

"Okay." She followed me out the door with her new pet in hand.

Downstairs the others had stirred. Dad and Petra were like two little kids shaking shit under the tree to see if they could guess what it was. Every year it's the same thing with these two. My older brother Julius and his bitch girlfriend Melanie weren't here this year thank shit. They were visiting her family who lived in Italy of all places, for the season. I'll miss my bro, but couldn't say I was sad to see the bitch queen go.

"Mom. Dad's shaking stuff again!" I told on his ass.

"Snitch!" He rubbed the top of my head like I was six, making the girls laugh and Tinks yip her ass off.

"Thaddeus get in here and leave that stuff alone. We'll open gifts early this year, right after brunch."

"Brunch, but I 'm hungry now, whatever happened to breakfast?" I grouched on the way to the kitchen.

"You be quiet and put on this apron..."

She got cut off which could only mean one thing; he was kissing the hell out of her. My parents did that a lot, nasty.

We spent the morning playing with the dog. Well, the girls spent the morning playing with the dog I watched them from my place on the couch, while mom and dad cooked away in the kitchen. Mom has this thing about preparing holiday meals on her own, whatever works. Us kids usually had KP duty at the end of the day to make up for it. Vicki seemed happy enough, she loved that stupid dog I could tell. Then again knowing her penchant for dogs...geez dude it's Xmas give it a rest. For just one day give it a rest, don't let that douche destroy today too.

Dinner was amazing as always. We were all stuffed to the gills and since mom had pulled a fast one we didn't end up opening gifts until afterwards. The blinking lights on the tree, which had been off all day until now had Tinks in a tizzy. When giftwrap paper was discarded she was in dog heaven. I just shook my head my kid was not too bright.

Vicki oohed and ached over her gifts, she got some kind of fancy ass watch from mom, a date just, whatever the fuck that is. It was pretty though, had some sort of flowers and shit made out of diamonds on the gold strap.

Dad gave her a new Birkin bag, correction, mom got her a bag and stuck dad's name on it. I'm sure my old man didn't know the first thing about these things.

"Lame dad, you know mom totally picked that stuff." I teased him out of earshot of the others.

"Dude I totally chose those out of a magazine, I even chose the colors, each of the girls got one this year."

"What, bargain basement shopping, two for one?"

"You're an idiot."

"Takes one old man."

"Natalia, your son is picking on me again."

"Roman leave your dad alone, you know how he gets at Xmas, he's worst than a toddler. And Thaddeus please stop whining."

"Hey, he started it." My dad is a real tool.

I was enjoying the easiness of the day. For the first time in what felt like months I could relax, I didn't feel the need to be on alert. My girl was happy as fuck and she hadn't even gotten all my gifts yet. I think she thought Tinks was her only gift this year.

The women raked it in this year like they did every year. Dad and I got mom and Petra tennis bracelets from Cartier with dinner rings, whatever the fuck that meant. The sales lady told us that they matched or some such shit.

Dad got new equipment for his home-clinic as we liked to call it. It was his own personal lab, which he'd set up for us to do research. Mom said we could do it as long as we didn't burn her house down.

I got a new Land Rover to go with my Ducati and Aston, sweet.

After things quieted down and my new offspring had tired herself out we headed back upstairs.

"Here Roman, these are for you." She was always shy when giving me gifts because she thought they weren't as extravagant as the ones my family gave. I've tried explaining to her that

that's just the way we are, we see something, we like it we get it. With the kind of money we had floating around we could have Xmas everyday and still not run through it all.

I opened my gifts all excited and shit, because what she failed to understand was that when it came from her it really was the thought that count for me. She got me some new kickass Ray Bans and a new Mariners hat, white with tiny blue stripes, sweet.

"Hey this is great baby thank you, I love them." She blushed and hung her head.

"Now you."

"What? I thought Tinks was my gift." Yeah like I'd give my girl a dog for Xmas and nothing else.

"Come 'ere and open these." I had three boxes for her.

"These two are for everyday wear nothing too extravagant I promise, you can wear it to school and shit. " She opened the first box and went goo goo over the silver Tiffany toggle necklace, that's what it was called I think. In the other box was the matching bracelet. She put them on right away. I don't know how well they would go with her new Rolex, freaking mom had to show me up.

The last box held her set from Cartier, a tennis bracelet just like mom and Petra's. Only her diamonds were in the shape of flowers, her dinner ring too was one big flower shaped entirely out of diamonds and the necklace to match.

"Oh Roman these are amazing, thank you."

"Why the fuck are you crying?" I pulled her onto my lap rocking her back and forth. She sniffled into my neck. I hated to fucking see her cry. I don't care if they were happy tears or not, I didn't trust that shit, I hated tears on her face. I tapped her ass gently.

" Cut it out sweet cheeks. Go clean your face we have to go take that plate to the station for your dad."

"Okay, be right back." She kissed me, well pecked was more like it before scurrying off to the bathroom.

We left the dog with mom and Petra and headed out in my new jeep. I think this is what I'd get her to drive, a matching one. His and Hers and maybe with some custom plates, sweet.

When we got to the station I almost lost my shit. What the fuck was he doing here? Couldn't I just enjoy one day without this motherfucker fucking it up? Vicki tensed like a springboard next to me and didn't move to get out of the car.

"Let's go." I got out and walked around to her side to let her out. She had her head down like she was hiding or some shit.

"Head up Victoria-Lynn." I ordered her, just like that my good mood was erased all the laughter and fun of the day was just sucked right out of me.

I kept my hand on her elbow as we headed up the stairs. The dog pulled away from the side of the building and made as if to approach her. I kept my mouth shut long enough to see what she would do.

"Vicki. Vicki." He called her name but she kept looking ahead not acknowledging his presence. Okay so far do good. Then the asswad reached out as if to touch her and I really lost it.

My fist was in his face before I knew I was going to do it. I didn't just stop there either I just kept pounding away on his fucking head. There was a ringing in my ears and a veil over my eyes. I didn't see or hear shit, just felt. I think Vicki was screaming for me to stop but I can't be sure.

Next thing I knew the sheriff and one of his deputies were there holding us apart. I guess the mutt had gotten in a few because my ribs hurt, but I'm declaring myself the winner because his shit was kinds a fucked up.

"What the hell is going on out here?" I ignored the Sheriff and focused on the douche. "Don't put your fucking hands on her again, next time you won't get off so lucky. Here you go sheriff." I took the package mom had packed from Vicki's hands that were shaking like fuck and gave it to him before turning and walking away.

"Vicki?" Her father called out to her.

"It's okay dad, I'll see you at home later."

No she won't. It was going to take a lot to calm me the fuck down, and I knew no better place to work off this energy than between her legs.

Chapter 12

ROMAN

I was fucking fuming on the way home. Rationally I knew this wasn't really her fault, but a part of me still fucking blamed her. I told her in the beginning; I fucking told her that guy was after more than friendship, but did she listen? Fuck no. Now I had to deal with this shit.

I pulled off onto a dirt road about ten minutes from home. I didn't even turn off the jeep, just jumped out, opened her door, pulled her the fuck out and pushed her against the hood face down. I fought with the zipper on her jeans until I got them opened, I pulled them down to her knees and pushed them the rest of the way with my foot.

I didn't take my pants off, just opened up, took my dick out and went to work. She was barely ready for me. I hadn't taken the time to prep her, but by stroke three she was with me. I grunted like a fucking beast as I pounded out my frustration on her pussy. One hand held her head down while the other used her hip to pull her back and forth, she was keening and trying to climb the hood but she wasn't getting away.

"Stay right the fuck there." I growled at her ass. I knew I was hurting her I wanted to fucking hurt her. It's her fault I was feeling this way, she could fucking deal.

"Please Roman I'm sorry, please."

"Shut, The Fuck, Up." I kept pounding away, my thrusts racing against the anger in my head and the pain in my heart. I came so fucking hard I went blind. I didn't give a fuck if she came or not, I was back to being mad as fuck.

Don't fucking judge me. You try dealing with this fuckery. One day you're happy as fuck, all's right in your world and then you come upon your significant other in a clinch with someone else, out in the open no less for the whole fucking world to see.

"Stop crying Vicki, you know I didn't really fucking hurt you, I've fucked you harder than that on a good day."

"Yes but you weren't using it as punishment then." She wiped her face.

"What the fuck do you expect? If you hadn't encouraged this shit he wouldn't think it's okay to put his fucking hands on you in front of me."

"I didn't..."

"Yes you fucking did." I yelled at her as I fixed my clothes, and she was slowly putting her clothes back in order.

"Every time I told you about that guy you played me with that friends bullshit. I'm a guy I know the fucking signs, you're supposed to be my fucking woman, but when it came to your relationship with him I had no say, you called the shots and look where that got us. Now you want me to go back to that? Fuck that, I'm through being your fucking chump."

"You're not..."

"Shut the fuck up. You know that's exactly what you took me for. That's why you strung me along for two fucking months while you ran around with him while freezing me the fuck out. I'm not your bitch Victoria-Lynn and no one fucks me if there's any fucking to be done I'll do the fucking. Now get in the fucking car." She had the good sense to shut the hell up and get in the car.

"Do you want me to take you home or are you coming home with me?"

"Home with you."

"Good, and none of that sulking shit, I told you how it was gonna be deal with it."

"But Roman you can't keep getting this angry about the same thing all the time. When are you gonna get over it? Am I gonna pay for one stupid mistake for the rest of my life?"

"Did you just tell me to get over it?"

"No, I asked how long before you get over it? That's not the same thing."

"Well Victoria-Lynn you might not have to pay for it for the rest of your life, but you will pay for it for as long as it takes me to get over the sight of YOU FUCKING KISSING HIM WITH HIS HANDS ON YOUR MOTHERFUCKING ASS."

I think she got the picture now.

Chapter 13

ROMAN

I was fucking furious when we got home. I barely said two words when we went through the doors. I think I heard my father mutter an' uh oh what happened now?' I didn't stop to find out, just got the fucking dog and took both of them upstairs.

"You're spoiling your family's Christmas."

"Yeah! Well mine is totally fucked." I threw my new hat on the bed.

"Am I sleeping on the bed because if I'm not then I'll just have Petra take me home." Oh she wanted to play? Okay I like that shit.

"Try it."

"Stop threatening me and stop being an asshole, I'm here aren't I? If you're gonna stay angry all the time I might as well not be here." I walked over to where she was hovering near the door. After slamming that shit shut I backed her up to the wall with my hand around her fucking throat.

"Who the fuck are you talking to?" She swallowed and wrapped her hands around mine.

"Do you think this is a fucking joke? Do you think because I love you that I'm soft, stupid or both? Answer me when I'm fucking talking to you." You need to calm the fuck down Blair, just walk away before you do something stupid. Shut the fuck up I'm not gonna hurt her, not really anyway. "I can't talk with your hand around my neck."

Shit. I dropped my hand but stayed in front of her. "I don't think it's a joke I just think you're blowing things out of proportion." I slammed my fist into the wall and stepped away. She still didn't get it; what the fuck?

"You weren't saying that shit when you ignored my ass for two fucking months over something that never happened."

"Not that again. Stop beating a dead horse." She walked over and plopped down on my bed.

"Get the fuck off my bed."

"No." She fucking igged me.

"Victoria-Lynn I 'm not playing with you."

"Come and make me." Oh she wanted to play.

"And what about you kissing that skank Tiffany?"

"We weren't together so that shit has nothing to do with you."

"You're an ass."

"Watch your mouth."

She kissed her teeth at me, what was I going to do with this girl? She doesn't listen for shit. I knew that passive shit wasn't going to last too long, she's always been stubborn as fuck.

I pulled on her feet to pull her off the bed and she kicked me. So I jumped her and squished her body under mine. She tried fighting me off but I trapped both her legs with mine and held her hands over her head.

"What now hot shot?" She tried to head butt my ass.

"I see you didn't learn your lesson." I flipped her over on the bed.

"Don't you dare, I'll scream the house down"

"Go ahead I don't care. If you want every one to know you're getting your ass spanked go ahead and scream."

"Roman I'm warning you."

I ignored her and brought my hand down on her jean clad ass. Hard.

She screamed and squirmed. I gave her a few more good smacks and then climbed off her.

She wiggled that shit at me, see, no respect at all.

"Kiss it and make it better." I got right on that.

Thank heavens the dog slept through the whole thing; Vicki was a freak. I think my punishment backfired on me though cause she wore my ass out.

Chapter 14

Victoria-Lynn

I think Roman lost his damn mind, seriously. I've never seen anything like it. The man went from knight in shining armor, to psycho asshole, all because of one stupid kiss. What would he do if he knew half the shit Timothy used to say?

See that's why I put up with his shit to a point, because I feel some guilt over that. He was right about Timothy wanting more, but I thought as long as I didn't that it would be okay. I thought I could handle the situation it isn't like I was trying to juggle two guys at once or anything.

Timothy was my friend since like gestation or something. How could I just cut him off ya know? But I guess I fixed my wagon but good; Because of that stupid kiss that didn't even amount to a hill a beans I no longer have a friend and I had this crazy ass man on my hands.

He knows I love him, I'm not going anywhere, he's just trying to see how far he can push, how much I'm willing to take. Don't get me wrong I know he's truly mad but I think most of it is still his pride; it'll wear off eventually. I hope it does soon because my kitty cat is sore. And here he comes again.

ROMAN

I had her call the sheriff and tell him she was spending the night. It wouldn't be the first time, but it was the first time we didn't use the guise of a sleepover with Petra. I could tell from her side of the conversation that he wasn't pleased. My raised eyebrow let her know I didn't give a fuck she was staying.

He was too late to play father, if he were any kinda father she wouldn't be running around kissing one man while being in an exclusive relationship with another.

You've really gone off the deep end haven't you Blair? Fuck you. Shit now I'm cussing myself.

"Open Sesame." Every time I felt myself getting mad I dove right back into her pussy. It was as if there was a direct line from my anger to my dick. She gave me a look but I didn't pay her any mind, I spread her open and sunk in to the hilt. Warm paradise.

I don't know what she was complaining about because every time I fucked her she was fucking right back at me, her hips never stayed still for a second. And begging me to fuck her harder didn't sound like a sore pussy to me. Whatever, her ass is gonna be ridden hard as fuck for at least a week. Hopefully I'd have worked off my mad by then.

I had to put the dog in her cage at some point cause she was getting way too interested in what was going on in the bed.

The bed was going sixty knots a minute and Vicki was moaning loud enough to wake the dead. Good times. See I knew this shit would calm me down. I never said only once would do it. Don't judge me because I might have just a tad bit more anger to work off than most.

"You better get use to this, for the rest of our lives every time you piss me off I'm gonna fuck you into submission."

"Bite me asshole."

"Okay."

I bit the shit outta the top of her cleavage. She did tell me to after all. She clamped down on my dick and tried to break my shit off, so I tweaked her clit until she came screaming.

"Bastard."

"Keep it up and I'll tan that ass again."

She kept quiet thank heavens. I was beat.

Chapter 15

ROMAN

The next day Vicki didn't want to go home so I left her and the dog with my mom and dragged dad out of the house with me.

"Where we going son?"

We climbed into my new ride. See that's the shit I love about my dad. He doesn't know where the fuck I was dragging him off to, but he was here, always had been.

"To the dealer, I need to get cheeks a new car."

"You two alright son? You seemed a little tense last night when you got back."

How do you tell your dad that your girl kissed another guy and you lost your shit?

"We're good, well we're going to be, nothing to worry about."

"Okay son, but you do know you can talk to me or your mother about anything that's bothering you right."

"Yeah dad I know."

This dealer we were going to was the shit, if we wanted something that was on the market overseas but not here yet he was the go to guy. My dad is a car freak he buys cars like other people buy newspapers. Funny thing is he drives every motherfucking one, except the collectibles, I think it was illegal to drive those or some shit.

At the dealers I made quick work of getting my girl the same jeep as mine, they were both midnight blue with ivory interiors. I got her all the bells and whistles just like mine, a cool hundred grand in less than ten minutes, don't tell me I don't love my girl. I would always give her only the best and I expect the same from her.

Dad drove my car back while I drove hers looking like a douche in a jeep with a big ass bow on it. What a sap.

I blew the horn when we got there and the girls came out with Tinks in tow.

Vicki's mouth dropped the fuck open when she saw her car, that's what I'm talking about. I bet she wasn't thinking about that piece a shit truck now.

That reminds me I need to call the local garage and have them tow that shit and scrap it. That's right I'm gonna obliterate the fuck out of it. I wonder if they'd let me operate the machine to crush the piece a shit. Or maybe I could take a sledgehammer to it and then have it delivered to that fuck's door.

Damn I'm a vengeful motherfucker. He deserves it though,

I'm gonna make him pay for that smirk for the rest of his natural born life. Kill the vendetta dreams pal here comes your girl.

"You like it baby?"

"Roman..." She face planted into my chest.

Why the fuck was she always crying when I did shit for her?

"I guess that means you like it, tomorrow we'll go get custom plates yeah?"

She nodded her head, good girl. I already knew exactly what those plates were going to say, she might not like it though, tough shit.

She put me in the position of having to prove some shit, and since she liked proving shit so much she should understand.

You're one twisted fuck you know that Blair? Fuck off asshole...wait, that's you you're talking to. I give a fuck.

Chapter 16

Victoria-Lynn

"Roman I can't drive around in car with POT DOC on it, my father is the sheriff."

"It means property of the doc, you'll have fun explaining it."

"Roman..."

"You can either have it as a license plate, or I can tattoo it on your ass, pick."

He'd gone off the deep end, that's all there is to it. How the hell do you reason with a crazy person?

"You're stuck on crazy you know that?"

"Whatever, get in the damn car." I just shook my head and got in, what else was there to do? I guess this was his idea of proving a point. Lord what have I started?

ROMAN

We went to pick up our new plates. Well to order them anyway, mine simply said THE DOC, while hers was a little more difficult. I wanted to spell the whole thing out but they said it was too many letters, shit. Well anyone with half a brain would figure it out. I don't know what she's griping about. At least it's better than my first inclination, which was having that shit tattooed on her damn forehead.

She'd spent the last two days at my house. Things were a little calmer but I was still pensive, like I was waiting for the next fuckery to jump off. Whatever it was I was ready for that shit. I'd had the heap a crap mobile towed, with the orders to seek and destroy. Good riddance to bad rubbish.

She wasn't too happy about that but one look and she piped the fuck down. She knew the deal.

I took her home so she could get her Christmas haul and pick up Tinks and all her shit; that dog was going to be spoiled. The two of them were cute as hell in the jeep though. I followed her to her house where the sheriff was sitting on the porch. He didn't look too happy but who gave a fuck?

"Hi dad." She kissed his cheek.

"Vicki, Blair."

"Sheriff." We had a mini stare down. I won.

"You wanna tell me what that was about on Xmas?"

"Crafton didn't tell you?"

"Nope, just said it was some sort of misunderstanding. He's okay by the way, nothing broken, in case you were wondering."

Oh he thought he was funny. "Not really no, can't say that I care one way or the other."

"Boy what the hell is your problem? You can't go around hitting people like that and in front of a police station no less."

I just looked at him, I hope he could read the message in my eyes. I do what the fuck I want.

"I don't want my daughter around that type of behavior."

Bring it the fuck on sheriff I dare you to go there.

"Dad it's not Roman's fault."

"You always stick up for him."

"Because it's the truth, maybe if I got a little more support from you regarding our relationship I wouldn't have been kissing Timothy...oh shit." She covered her mouth. I'm guessing she didn't mean to share that tidbit.

"What?" He looked back and forth between us in confusion. "Why would you do such a thing?"

I could see she was embarrassed as hell so I tried to divert the situation. I'm the only one allowed to make her sweat over this shit.

"It's okay sheriff we sorted it out."

He shook his head in disappointment, what the fuck? I thought he wanted those two together, at least that's the impression I always got.

"I thought I raised you better than that...your mother..."

Oh shit, Vicki's mother was a sore topic. She ran out on them when Vicki was too young to remember, to go live with another man.

"Dad, I'm nothing like Stephanie."

"Baby don't cry." I hugged her to me I hated fucking tears. The sheriff just got up and went inside. Fucking douche, he'd been throwing that guy at her all this time and now he had the nerve to act disappointed.

"Great, now my own father thinks I'm a whore."

"I'm sure he doesn't think that cheeks." What the hell do I know? The man's always been crazy.

"You do." She mumbled against my chest.

"I do what?"

"Think I'm a whore."

"Did I ever say that to you? Don't put words in my fucking mouth." Tink's started growling at my raised voice, I pointed my finger at her and she piped the fuck down.

"Then why?"

"You know why, now wipe your face and go talk to your dad."

"I wanna go back with you."

"I'll come get you later you haven't been home in a while and you know how he gets." I kissed her head and went back to my car. She was still standing there when I drove off.

I hope that fuck didn't say anything else to make her cry I didn't want to get into it with the sheriff but if he fucked with her I would. She was right too. Maybe if he'd supported our relationship instead of trying to shove the mutt down her throat she wouldn't have been so confused as to go kissing the douche.

Now he's really on my shit list.

Chapter 17

ROMAN

I wasn't too sure about leaving her there alone with him. I mean what the fuck! He'd all but called my girl a whore. And that shit about comparing her to her mother, not cool. I think I'm gonna give her two hours tops with that asshole and then go get her, I don't like the vibe I felt back there. If he fucks with her I know exactly what to do, and he wasn't going to like it one bit.

I'd barely reached my driveway before my phone rang; caller ID said sweet cheeks.

"Babe."

"Roman?"

I had no idea what the fuck she was saying, but I did know she was crying. I slammed my car back into drive and peeled the fuck off. I knew I shouldn't have left her there, what the fuck was I thinking?

I pulled up outside their house and could hear the screaming from the driveway. I didn't wait, just ran through the fucking door. Gun or not the sheriff wouldn't dare fuck with me my father would bury his ass.

"Vicki." She ran to me and I hugged her close. I don't think I'd allowed myself to think the whole way here as long as she was breathing I could deal with whatever.

"What're you doing here Roman? This is between me and my daughter.

I ignored his ass she was my only interest. I tried to raise her head from my chest but she stiffened so I used more force.

"The fuck." There was a red handprint on her cheek. I started to step toward him but she held on tight.

"No please, let's just go." I gave him a warning look. This shit wasn't over not by a long fucking shot. I grabbed Tinks and Vicki had her bags from earlier so we just left. I was fucking livid.

"Where do you think you're going Victoria Lynn get your ass back in here."

This asshole lost his fucking mind. "No Roman let's just go please." She pulled me around and towards my jeep. I put her in the passenger seat and belted her in. I held her face and looked the handprint and wanted to commit fucking homicide. I kissed her cheek as softly as I could before heading around to the driver's side. The motherfucker was standing on the porch fuming. If I had a gun handy I woulda popped him.

"We'll get you jeep later."

She didn't say a word, just cried her fucking eyes out, which was breaking my fucking heart. I didn't tell her to stop this time though. I had to think about what came next. I knew I should've followed my mind. Now look at this shit.

When we reached my house I carried her inside, mom and Petra came running when they saw me carrying her.

"Roman what's happened?"

"I don't know yet mom." I laid her out on the couch when what I really wanted was to carry her upstairs to sleep this shit off.

Mom ran to get dad because she was afraid Vicki was hysterical and I couldn't do anything but hold her, I didn't want to let her go long enough to play doctor.

Dad took one look at her face and turned an angry look my way. "Son?"

"What the fuck dad!"

"Okay, not you, who?"

"The sheriff."

Dad's face went stone cold, yeah dad's a scary motherfucker too. Where did you think I got it?

He whispered some shit in her ear that seemed to calm her down a little. She didn't say anything, just reached her hands up for me like a child. I picked her up, grabbed the dog and headed upstairs.

"Thanks guys I'll take it from here."

I took my girl and our dog up to my room and laid her on the bed, she was so fucked she wouldn't even let me go long enough to take off my shoes.

"Cheeks I'm not going anywhere I'm right here, let me just take off our shoes okay?" I had to use a soft voice and tender strokes of her hair to keep her calm. Whatever happened, if nothing else the sheriff was gonna pay for this shit. Fuck no he wasn't getting away with slapping her in the face. I hadn't slapped the shit out of her and I'm the one she did that shit to. No you just spit in her face, think that's any better? Shut the fuck up, she deserved it at the time.

I held her for the rest of the day and watched her hiccup and cry in her fucking sleep. Did I mention how much I hate fucking tears on her face? I wanted to go right now and beat the living shit out of that asshole, but the fact that she would wake alone held me back. She needed me here, besides we needed to make plans, I'd be fucked if she was going back to his house. Not if I had anything to say about it.

Chapter 18

ROMAN

After my girl cried her fucking self to sleep I went on a rampage. There were a few things I needed to discuss with my parents, only out of respect for them but one way or the other I would make this shit happen.

That motherfucker had no right. He was half a fucking father to begin with and that was being generous. She tried to hide that shit from me but I knew. I know what a real father is I have one.

This neglectful fuck first implied my baby was a whore and then put his motherfucking hands on her. Now I'm out for blood. It didn't matter that I'd been hard on her, what she'd done was fucked, but it was done to me. He had no reason for putting his fucking hands in her face.

I went down the stairs with Tinks in hand, I didn't want her waking up Vicki. Yeah you're attached to the damn dog. Would you shut the fuck up motherfucker? Damn.

My dad jumped on me as soon as I reached the landing.

"Roman what the hell is going on? And don't tell me it's nothing. First you've been like a bear with his paw caught for the past few weeks and we didn't see hide nor hair of Vicki in all that time. Then you took off for Portland with no explanation. Now you and Vicki are back together at least it looks that way. Now she shows up with her father's handprint in her face. Start talking son, are you two in some kind of trouble?"

"No dad, no one's in trouble, Vicki and I just had a misunderstanding, but I do need something from you."

"Name it son, anything."

"I want her to move in here with me. She's not going back to that fucking house, if we can't stay here I'll buy us a place, but I'd rather we stayed here."

"Okay."

"No questions asked?"

"Roman you're almost twenty-one Vicki's of age, you have a whole floor to yourself, I don't see why it should be a problem. Besides I wasn't too keen on her going back there to a man who slaps her in the face either. Your mother and I were trying to figure out what to do next. Discipline is one thing but to hit a child so hard you leave you palm in her face; that's a no no."

"Okay, next question, how do I bring him down?"

"Son."

"No dad, he's not getting away with that shit."

"Son, don't you think you're going a little overboard?"

"I don't think it's the first fucking time. There've been other times when she made excuses for shit and I just accepted her word because I couldn't believe...doesn't matter. I want him to pay, and since beating the fuck outta him would land me in more trouble than it would him, I have to find another way."

"Let's think about it some more son, he's still her father. Are you sure you want to go down that road?"

"Dad Vicki and I will always be solid no matter what."

"Well, if you're sure this is the way you want to go."

"I'm sure." Fuck yeah you piece a shit, I'll watch you bleed. Teach your ass to put hands on what's mine.

ROMAN

I stayed with her until she awakened with me and Tinks for company. Poor Tinks, I think she realized something was wrong with her mother because she was being extremely affectionate.

"You feeling better babe?" I pulled her on top of me so I could see her face.

"Uh huh." She was still fucking sniffling.

"Roman, do you think I'm a whore?" I'm gonna kill that mother-fucker.

"What did that fuck say to you?"

"I don't wanna say." She hid her face in my neck.

"Tell me." I shook her lightly.

"He called me a dirty little whore, just like my mom. He said I had no business being with you in the first place, but since I'd decided to sell my...you know what to the highest bidder, the least I could've done is not play the whore for the whole town to see." I was off the bed before she was done.

"No Roman don't, you can't, you'll get in trouble." She tried grabbing for me but I shook her off. I didn't hear, see, or feel, I was in a whole other zone.

The killing motherfucking zone. Fuck everything else.

She ran past me down the stairs screaming for my dad.

He met me on the landing with my brother who apparently arrived from Europe while we were upstairs. Didn't give a fuck about that now either. She was fucking crying uncontrollably, mom and Petra were wringing their hands, and dad and Julius were trying to diffuse the situation.

"The fuck outta my way Jules."
He pushed me back forcefully with
one hand on my chest. I didn't want to
fight with my brother but I would if I
have to, before I could take a swing
dad stepped in.

"Son we talked about this, you have to
calm down."

"Dad you know what the fuck he said
to her?"

"That doesn't matter right now. Do you
want to end up in jail for assaulting a
man of the law? Do you know the shit
storm that would follow your actions?
Who's going to protect her then, when
you're in fucking prison?"

"What the fuck is going on?"

I'd forgotten that Jules hadn't been
around for all the fuckery. I'm glad his
bitch of a girlfriend wasn't here
because her constant fucking
annoyance would be the last fucking
thing I need right now, bitch always
had something fucked to say.

"Apparently Kenneth hit Victoria-Lynn." Dad gave up the information.

I heard Jules draw in a deep breath.

Now see my brother loves the fuck outta my girl, I don't know what the fuck it is with them though I'm glad of it.

They're thick as fucking thieves. Unless the bitch queen was in attendance, she couldn't stand Vicki, but Julius loved his lil sis as he was fond of calling her.

He picked her up now hugging her tightly as he whispered something in her ear. She put her head down on his shoulder still fucking crying. Him and our dad were the only two men who could get away with that shit, I didn't even like the sheriff doing that shit and now I see it was with good reason, the fuck.

I wasn't exactly calm, but dad had a point. If I got into that kind of trouble not only would I fuck my future in the medical profession, but it would interfere with my ability to be here for her, and she fucking needed me. I'll deal with my own shit later.

He needed to be dealt with but right now she came first.

When Jules released her she flew into my arms. I kissed her hair to let her know everything was okay for. She'd had enough for one day. I'll save my crazy for later but this shit was on.

"Please don't do anything stupid Roman, please." She clutched at me as I held her tighter.

"I'll make sure he stays put baby sis, don't worry about it." He ruffled her hair as he inclined his head to me, which meant he wanted a word in private.

I passed my girl off to my mom and sister for safe keeping after whispering reassurances in her ear. I followed my father and brother from the room. Some shit women just don't need to know about. Especially nosy ass mom, she likes to diffuse shit. As soon as we were out of sight of them my brother turned and glared at me. "How the fuck did you let this shit happen?"

"I wasn't there bro, he waited until I left. The fuck."

"This the first time?" Right to the point, that's what I'm talking about.

"I don't think so but I'm waiting for her to calm down so I can get to the bottom of it."

"Fair enough." He went to get a drink leaving me alone with dad.

"Dad where do we stand if I go after him? He might put up a fight about her staying here and I'm telling you now she's not going back."

"Kenneth Baldwin knows better than to fuck with me and mine son. Let's just wait and see what he does next."

"Fuck waiting. He gets to pay for this shit, your words dad, remember? Vicki belongs to Roman, someone put hands on her he has to stand up." Jules came out of the kitchen with a juice bottle and a scowl.

"But this is her father."

"Your point?"

Fuck If Jules went on the warpath the sheriff is so fucked. "I get first dibs bro, my girl."

Chapter 19

ROMAN

I had to tell them everything but I told it from Vicki's point of view, her version of events leading up to the kiss.

Julius looked ready to go beat the shit out of Crafton for putting her in that position in the first place. I was down with that, but dad was watching us like we were adopted miscreants.

"What the hell did your mother raise?" Whatever. He kept saying shit like that each time we threw an idea out there. I don't know what he expected us to do with the fucks. Have tea?

"So, how're we going at this fuck bro?" See, my brother knows me very well.

"I'm not sure yet but I do know anyone as fucked up as he is, must have skeletons in their closet. I plan on finding every last one and using them to bury the fuck."

"Good thinking bro, I'll start digging, by the time we're through with his abusive ass he wouldn't know what the fuck hit him, you're not sending her back there right?"

"Fuck no, she ain't ever going back if I have anything to say about it. Speaking of which, I need to go get the rest of her shit and her new jeep."

"We'll all go, I don't think it's a good idea for you to be alone with the sheriff." Dad was such a worrier.

We kicked around ideas for a while, all of which dad found fault with in between bemoaning us as criminals.

Jules wanted to beat the shit out of the sheriff, which was my number one favorite. Either that he said or pay someone else to do it, whichever way works for me but dad forbid it.

I left them and went in search of my girl. We had a few things to hash out. She was in the living room with my mom, sis and Tinks. I just picked her up and headed upstairs with her after thanking the others for watching over her for me.

I wasn't too fucking happy to see tear tracks still on her face but I guess she had to get it all out of her system.

"Babe you know I'm not letting you go back there right? There's no debate on that, you're staying here. If you want to see that fucker you can see him when I'm there but you're not staying in that house with him."

"Roman we talked about this and..."

"Which part of no discussion didn't you get babe? End of fucking discussion, now all I need to know is what the fuck you want from there?"

"I'll have to come with you, all my stuff is there, my whole life."

"No, your fucking life is here, those are just things, I'd rather you left all that shit there, everything he paid for at least."

"Roman be reasonable, I can't just pretend my dad doesn't exist he made a stupid mistake..."

"Save that shit, even when I was angry as fuck at you I didn't hit you."

"You spanked me."

"During sex, two completely different things, and believe me I wanted to belt you one, but I had enough control not to go through with that shit Victoria-Lynn. He hit you so hard he left his print in your fucking face, it's a wonder he didn't break your fucking face."

"Okay calm down baby."

"Don't tell me to calm down when you compare what I did to what that fuck did, not cool babe."

"Okay, I get it, I do."

Did she really think I would hit her like that? Okay I admit I was a fucking lunatic the last little while, but I hadn't let myself go too far. I'd much rather beat the fuck outta that piece a shit Crafton than hit her like that.

"Tomorrow we're getting your shit, I think Jules and dad are going, dad seems to think I mean your father harm."

"I think you're blowing this whole thing out of proportion, dad will be fine by now and full of apologies."

"Does this a lot does he?"

"No, dammit that's not what I meant."

She was fucking lying. I'm going to fuck him up, but for now I'll leave it alone. No use in stressing her more than she already was.

I started tuning her up so we could both forget this shit for a while. "Go to your room Tinks. Daddy wants to violate mommy this isn't for you." The damn dog gave me the stink eye before whining and heading for her little bed. It's a shame that the dog's only been here a few days and she already knows what I was up to.

I finally turned my attention to my girl and kissed the ugly mark on her face. Mom had done some shit to it to make the swelling go down but it was still bad. "Does it still hurt baby or did dad's cream help?"

"It only stings a little it at least it's not throbbing so much any more." I wanted to fucking punch the living shit out of something or someone. She must've seen my intentions on my face because her legs came up around me. I looked down at her gorgeous face. "I'm not sure this is such a good idea anymore baby. I need to pound something and you're already bruised and battered. I don't think your little pussy can handle this heat." I pressed my cock into her covered pussy so she'd have an idea. There were times when my dick for some unknown reason would get harder and longer than others. I don't question the shit I just go with it. this was one of those times. I'm not sure if was the anger or adrenaline that did I, usually it was her mouth wrapped around it but what the fuck.

"I'd rather you pound me than to go get into trouble." I ran my hand down her middle until I reached the hem of her skirt. She was wearing sexy as silk thongs. I pulled those shit down and tossed them. Raising her skirt I studied her waxed plump pussy lips. Fuck, go easy Blair. Yeah okay. I licked her just the outside of her pussy first, until her juices started coming and then I pushed my tongue in little by little teasing the fuck out of her while thumbing her clit. I know that shit makes her crazy. When she was nice and primed I worked two fingers inside her ass while I tongue fucked her. I needed her to cum hard and fast because I needed to fuck. When she gushed into my mouth that was my cue. I reared up between her thighs and grabbing them, pushed them back to her ears leaving her pink pussy open for my cock. I watched as it slid into her like a heat seeking missile. "Hold on baby." That was all the warning she got before I slammed that rest of the way home. Balls deep and still I wanted to be deeper. I pulled back and did my nine short one long technique. I needed her pussy wet and open because I could feel that need snapping at me. If I fucked her the way I wanted to and she wasn't turned way the fuck on I'd hurt her for sure. By the third round of seven short three long she was panting for my cock. And I let go. I pounded into her so hard her whole body shook, still she asked for more. Fine, I guess my girl needed it hard too. After I'd made her cum twice with her knees up by her ears I pulled out and flipped her over. "Head down pussy in the air." She assumed the position and held onto the headboard. I rubbed my cock head up and down her weeping pussy slit before slipping back inside. With her ass held firmly in both hands I plowed into her. "Fuck, tell me if I hurt you." She shook her head wildly and pushed back against me.

"No it feels good don't stop." It wasn't long before the only sounds in the room were the creaking of the bed and our combined moans as her ass slapped back into my forward thrusts. I bit into her neck when she squeezed down on my cock and emptied my nuts inside her. "Round one." I planned on keeping her busy for the rest of the day and night. We could deal with the bullshit tomorrow.

ROMAN

A caravan followed us to her old house. Why my whole family including my mom and my sister felt the need to come with me to get her shit was beyond me but they insisted.

My girl was back to being scared, I'd tried to fuck the fear out of her since she insisted she had to come with and it had worked too. Until we turned the corner to her old house and she was back to biting her lip and fiddling with the ends of her shirt.

I didn't like her biting her lip unless she was doing it while riding me.

"Stop worrying you think I'm gonna let him do anything to you?"

"No it's not that, I just hate confrontation, and now your whole family is here. It was just one little slap Roman really, there's no need to make all this fuss."

"Babe, seriously? We've been all through that already you're not gonna change my mind you're staying with me. No one is putting their fucking hands on you again I don't care who the fuck it is."

I turned away to let her know I was finished with the conversation.

We pulled into the driveway and the sheriff came out with a beer. He sent my woman a look that if my family hadn't been there would've had me going for his throat. Piece a shit. I made to walk right by him but he stopped me.

"What do you think you're doing?"

"It would behoove you to get the fuck outta my face."

"Roman..." Dad started with his warning tone shit, he had no idea how much control it was taking not to fucking knock this dick's head off.

I kept going, wishing he would put his hands on me, but of course the punk did nothing but watch me walk into his house.

I headed up the stairs to her room knowing she was safe with my family but she was soon behind me. I heard raised voices downstairs but ignored them.

"Get your stuff babe and lets get the hell outta here, the less time I spend around your father the better.

She went around the room gathering what she wanted to take with her.

"Victoria-Lynn get down here."

"Ignore him, he's drunk."

That seemed to make her more nervous and thinking about the reason for that nervousness only pissed me off more.

When she was ready we walked back downstairs where there seemed to be some kind of standoff going on. Dad was standing in front of mom and Petra while Julius was slightly off to the side body thrust forward like he was ready for anything.

"You're not taking my daughter anywhere, that's kidnapping."

"And you call yourself the sheriff, it's not kidnapping if she comes voluntarily."

"She can't go anywhere voluntarily she's still a minor."

"Not in this state she's not, and if you think I would leave her here alone with you after what you did then you must be a bigger asshole than I thought."

I held her hand and led her away from him. He made a grab for her and caught my fucking fist, or he would've if fucking Jules hadn't grabbed me around my middle pulling me back.

He made as if to hit me, but dad had had enough.

"Put your hands on my kid Kenneth and you'll have a shit load of problems you won't believe. Also know this, I have documented proof that you abused your daughter. You might want to sober up and think about that before you make any more moves. Let's go boys."

Mom had already taken the girls outside, he started to say something else but I just looked his ass dead in the eyes.

"You ever think of touching her again I'll fuck you over, father or not."

"She's my daughter, you can't tell me what to do with my daughter."

"She's mine now, you're done."

I left and went to get my girl and take her the fuck home. Julius hopped into her jeep and we headed out.

Tinks was losing her fucking mind when we got back. I guess in all the chaos we forgot the poor thing.

Vicki gave her some love before I put her in the bathroom, I needed some fucking love, my adrenaline was pumping like a son of a bitch and since I didn't get to deck her douche of a father I had to expend that shit somehow, I knew just how to do it.

I picked her tiny ass up, pulled her pants down her legs, laid her back on the bed and attacked her pussy with my mouth.

I felt like a fucking animal, I just wanted to devour her.

"Oh, oh." Her eyes rolled back in her head, that's right baby enjoy.

When I was done making her come in my mouth I flipped her over.

"This is going to be quick and rough babe."

I slammed into her body making her jerk and clutch the sheets in her fists.

"Mine, mine, mine...fucking mine, always." I pounded into her like a man possessed. Like I hadn't spent last night buried inside her. "Say it." I bit her back hard enough to draw blood. I was a mad man I couldn't stop. I needed to consume her.

"I'm yours, only yours."

"That's right baby, I'm going deeper, take it."

I raised her hips off the bed and pounded into her with force. I watched my cock as it went in and out of her completely covered in her pussy juice.

"So fucking good baby, so fucking sweet, no one else, ever, no one will ever touch you like this but me, I'd kill you first."

I really meant that shit, this was it, no going back for either of us. I'd taken her out of her father's house; she was now wholly my responsibility. I would do a better job in the future of taking care of her so assholes didn't take advantage of her.

After almost mauling her I spent the rest of the day loving her gently, reaffirming my love for her. Seems like the last month or so had been nothing but fuckery, I'm gonna change that shit starting now. We cuddled close with the damn dog in the middle of us giving me looks. "She was mine first fur ball." The fuck.

Chapter 20

ROMAN

So far Jules and I have been coming across some crazy shit where one sheriff Baldwin is

Concerned. The most disturbing being the fact that no one else has ever seen or heard from his wife since she supposedly left in the middle of the night. I haven't been sharing anything we've found so far with sweet cheeks, she gets way too emotional when it comes to her father and their fight. I don't care what she says she's not seeing him without me. And I'm not ready to look at him without fucking him up.

It's been two weeks since she moved in with me, two weeks of

158 | JORDAN SILVER

nonstop loving and playing, just being
a young couple in love again I guess. I
hardly ever remember being mad at
her and why, but on those rare
occasions that I do, I fight it back,
she's my baby again. She needs me to
protect her more than she needs my
anger. I still don't like that shit and NO
I haven't necessarily forgiven the
fuckery yet either, but nothing's going
to stop me from loving my girl, she's
still my heart. Spoilt ass. Her and the
damn dog think they own me. I can't
make a move without one or the other
of them in my arms. At least she's
getting over that shit with her father
and mom and dad acts like she's lived
here her whole life so it's made
settling in easier. I try not to fuck her
every time I look at her but it's close. I
let her up to eat and spend at least an
hour with mom and sis. What the fuck!
I still have shit to work off, maybe it's
not anger anymore; I call it the
bonding season.

Now this fuckery is going in a whole other direction than I expected. I wanted to find some dirt, like maybe unlawful arrests or shit like that, just something to put his ass in the hot seat. So far we'd found that and more. Kenneth Baldwin is a sick fuck. It made me sick to think that my girl was under his sole care all these years with no one to intervene. There were no aunts and uncles, and no grandparents in the picture.

Him and his friend Stephen Crafton the mutt's father seemed to be into some sick shit that involved of all things setting up hunting expeditions in the deep woods that surround our town. It wasn't the hunting that was the problem. It's what we suspect they were hunting. If what we had uncovered was true these fucks were hunting humans. We'd found some graphs and charts. Yes Jules had put his hacking skills to work regardless of what dad had said. When we matched up the charts and graphs against missing persons reports going back almost fifteen years the story they told was horrifying. On paper at least it seemed like they were being paid some very big bucks by some very twisted fucks with money, some of them well known, to capture and release people in the forest to be hunted like wild animals. Oh yeah they had all that shit documented.

"Fuck Jules, what the fuck did we stumble onto here?" I ran my hand over my face my only thought of her.

"I don't know bro, one thing's for sure, lil sis can never be left alone with that fuck ever again."

"You don't have to tell me that bro, she's already been told. I'm not telling her about any of this shit though, not until we know for sure, and this shit with her mom; I'm gonna get Marcus on it, see if there's any trace of her. I hope like fuck she's alive somewhere and is just a fucked up mother. My girl spent her whole life hating her because that dick put it in her head that her mom didn't want her, that she abandoned her. Imagine the guilt she'll feel if that shit turns out to be a lie. It'll fucking devastate her.

"I gotta say bro from everything we've learned so far, I'm thinking she's not among the living anymore."

"What I don't get is why no one questioned his version of events." I shook my head, pissed way the fuck off, this shit was just gonna set her back.

"He's the sheriff bro, okay back then he wasn't, but he was on the fast track, who was gonna believe one of their own upstanding citizens could be guilty of such a fucked up thing. Besides he's a cop, he knows the ins and outs of their investigations. It wouldn't take much to plant the seeds. Just drop a word here and there, you know, the old, my wife isn't happy, I think my wife is cheating, shit like that, get a sympathetic ear, then one day you just say the bitch left in the middle of the night, who's gonna doubt you?"

"That's fucked Jules, this whole fucking thing is fucked."

"Well the good thing is we got her outta there, one less worry. Now all we gotta do is bring this fuck down. The thing is though, we're gonna need dad on this shit."

"Fuck, he's gonna pitch a fucking fit. You wish we'd a left shit alone?"

"Fuck no little brother, who knows what he would've ended up doing to her if we hadn't intervened when we did, the sick fuck."

"He's never getting anywhere near her again no way." I'll be back later I need a break from this fuckery. Besides it's almost time for dinner."

I went in search of my girl, lately if she wasn't hanging with Petra, she could be found playing with Tinks out on the lawn.

School had started back and so had my internship so we were both rather busy, but never too busy for each other.

In the evenings when her homework was done and I happened to be home, we would curl up together in my room and watch TV, or join the family downstairs. That's when I wasn't buried inside her.

We all usually ate dinner together that was mom's thing meals had to be together, which was usually a light, jovial, atmosphere. Except on those occasions when Melanie came over.

"What you doing baby?" She was laying on her back in our bed staring up at Tinks.

"We're having a staring contest, she's being a very bad girl."

"Oh yeah, what'd she do?" These two were too fucking cute it makes me smile.

"She tried to eat my chucks, bad Tinks." I scratched the spoilt pooch behind the ears before planting a long hot wet one on my baby. "It's time for dinner babe."

"Is Melanie gonna be here?" She sounded...off, which had my hackles rising.

"What the fuck, who gives a fuck? She say some shit to you?"

"No, not really, it's just... she makes me feel I like don't belong here."

"What the fuck did I tell you? Someone say some shit to you, you tell me about it right away, no fucking games. Now what the fuck did that bitch say?"

She looked at me all mutinous like, like she wasn't gonna answer me and shit. She knew better.

"Victoria-Lynn..." Good, now we were having a staring contest. I won.

"Oh alright, she just said something about me not fitting in here, that I'm ...different, my background, and all this new trouble with me and my dad..."

"The fuck?" I grabbed her hand and pulled her out the room. I'm gonna nip his shit in the bud once and for all. With everything that I'd learned in the past few days my girl was gonna need all the support she could get. She damn sure didn't need anyone tearing her down. Besides I needed an outlet for all the anger building inside of me. This bitch was just the right one to feel my wrath.

I found her in the kitchen sitting at the island. Perfect, everyone was here, including my dad. I walked right up to her with Vicki in tow. Jules must've seen the thundercloud on my face because he tried to intercept me. No dice.

"Listen here bitch, if you ever in your life disrespect her again, I'll forget that you mean something to my brother and lay you the fuck out, you get me?"

"Roman what in the world are you doing son?"

"No disrespect dad but this piece a shit does not get to make Vicki feel unwanted in her own home, no one does. She's family, she's my fucking family. If she's made to feel unwelcome then we'll both leave."

"Son take it easy, let's try to get to the bottom of this in a calm manner."

"Mom you've been there, we've all been there when she makes her little snide remarks. I let that shit slide because of you Jules, but that shit is dead and you know why. Anyone fucks with her they'll deal with me." My girl was fucking shaking, no fucking way.

"What did you do Melanie?" Jules was getting pissed; he knew I would never go after her like this unless it was bad.

"Nothing, I have no idea what he's talking about, if his little girlfriend lied and told him..."

"Fuck you bitch, you're doing it again, now you're calling her a fucking liar. She didn't even want to tell me what the fuck you said."

"What did she say son?"

"Go on Vicki, tell dad what she said to you."

"Roman...no." She whispered that shit like a little kid who was afraid of getting into trouble. With everything I now knew about her father and what must've been a fucked up home life still fresh on my mind, that shit just made me that much angrier.

"You can speak up baby, there's no need to fear her, I'm right here." She hung her fucking head, hiding behind her hair.

"She said I should go back home, that I didn't fit in here, my family background isn't like the rest of yours." She spoke really softly but we all heard her.

"Oh Melanie, how could you?" Mom came over and hugged Vicki while Petra gave Melanie the death glare.

Jules was too pissed to speak so he just glared as well. The proud bitch didn't even have the decency to apologize she just looked straight ahead. Dad came over and brushed her hair, my poor baby. What the fuck?

"Victoria-Lynn I hope you know that no one in this family thinks that way about you. When my son brought you home to us it was with the understanding that you were someone very special to him, and that's the vein in which you were received . Since then we've all grown to love you not just because of Roman, but because of who you are. I'm sorry that anyone made you feel

less than welcomed in my home. From Natalia and myself I offer you my humble apologies and promise that this will never happen again." This last was said while looking at Melanie, who was finally looking properly chastened.

"I think you need to leave Melanie."

"Julius..." She wasn't too happy with that shit. Jules was always very catering to her trifling ass, don't know what he sees in the slag but hey, to each his own.

"No, I'll talk to you later, if I say anything to you right now it won't be pretty. I told you about this shit before. Roman is my brother and Vicki is my lil sis you don't fuck with either of them. If you can't get that through your head then you're not welcomed here. I'll see you at your place or when we go out, but that shit you pulled was fucked up. I'm very disappointed in you, come on let's go, I'll walk you out."

I wanted to kick the bitch on her way out but from the looks of her she was already feeling pretty low. Serves her ass right.

"Now I feel bad." Cheeks hid her face in my side.

"No reason to feel bad baby, this is your home not hers, you live here, she visits. Now she'll think twice before fucking with you again. Next time I won't be so easy on her ass. Now I'm hungry let's eat." I give a shit about that bitch.

For the rest of the night everyone was extremely nice to my girl, especially Jules. We were all trying to make her feel better about the whole situation. I'm sure there had been more said because Melanie is a psychotic bitch but I'm on it now. There will be no more of that shit.

That night when I took her upstairs I wanted to be gentle with her, in fact I started out that way. I kissed from her toes to her neck, soft, gentle, loving nips. "Damn babe, what the hell did you put on your skin?" She smelt and felt fucking amazing.

"Something Natalia bought me you like it?" It tasted like fucking peaches or some shit.

I sucked her nipples until they were red and swollen, making her squirm and try to get my cock inside her pussy before I was ready.

"Wait baby." I kissed my way back down her body until I reached her core. The scent was stronger there near her waxed pussy. I ate her like a starving man, licking deep until her juices coated my tongue as I held her up to my mouth.

Fuck I wasn't going to be able to do gentle, I wanted to fuck her into the bed. She was pulling on my hair and mewling, begging me to come inside her. "Now Roman please." I licked her pussy one last time before raising up and fucking into her.

"Fuck babe." She raised her knees up to her chest and I slipped deeper. I used both hands to raise her ass up to meet my thrusts as I fucked her mouth with my tongue.

Her pussy was milking me already, greedy fuck. I rubbed the ridge of my dick against her clit with each stroke, which always made her cum screaming.

"I'm cumming, I'm cumming..."

"Cum all over my dick baby." I gave her a few hard strokes, which forced her deeper into the mattress as she flooded my dick and the bed with her juices.

I came like a fucking geyser while biting into her neck. She tightened even more drawing the last of my essence from me.

I pulled out and laid next to her drawing her into my arms, both of us trying to catch our breath.

"Oh shit, where's Tinks?"

"I think she knew what we were up to so she went into the bathroom with her toy."

"Thank fuck, you feeling better baby?"

She nodded against my shoulder. I kissed her brow, brushed her hair back and settled down. We'll get up later to take a shower right now I was bushed to move my ass. Tinks stuck her head out the bathroom door and I think the little shit rolled her eyes at me. "Come on you, and don't give me none of your shit." She came over to the bed and I picked her little ass up and dropped her on her mother. I settled down with my girls in my arms.

Fuck, how am I gonna deal with this shit with her father? Fuck.

Chapter 21

ROMAN

As soon as Vicki fell asleep I went in search of Jules. Melanie is a bitch yes, but she's the woman he loves, and though I could give a shit about her he's my heart ya know.

I found him in the media room playing one of those stupid ass video games. "Hey Jules."

"Hey lil bro, I thought you were asleep."

"I wanted to talk to you first. Listen I want to apologize for earlier, Melanie got what she deserved but that couldn't have been easy for you..."

"Stop right there bro, you have nothing to apologize for, Melanie was wrong right across the board, had no right to say that shit to lil sis. I wish I knew what the fuck her problem was though, jealousy maybe, but that's crazy right?"

"Who the fuck knows with females, it seems for some it doesn't matter how beautiful they are or how much nice shit they have there's always something the other one have that they want."

I shrugged my shoulders, I didn't give a shit what that bitch's issue was with my girl, just as long as she didn't fuck up again and caused me to do something that would hurt my brother.

"Besides, we got more important things to deal with right now." When Jules started cracking his knuckles and popping his neck somebody was about to get fucked up.

"What's up?" I dropped down beside him.

"That Timothy kid, what're we doing about him?"

"Well, I already put my foot up his ass. He knows to stay the fuck away from her, but we'll see how bright he really is."

"You think he knows what his father and the sheriff are into, maybe he's part of it?"

"I'm not sure, I hate his fucking guts, but Vicki keeps saying she's the one who initiated the kiss. Although she says he'd been pressuring her for more than friendship, so I don't know what kind a guy he really is, that's some twisted shit..."

"What about the other, what are we gonna do? We need a course of action, can't go off half cocked."

"I know. We need hard evidence but I can't seem to come up with how to get that shit. We'll figure it out though, no way we can let that shit go. You didn't tell dad did you?"

"Uh oh, what are you two up to over there?"

Dad came into the room and sat after ruffling our hair like we were five. "Hey hands off the hair pal."

"That shit's fucked already son."

Jules cracked the fuck up. Huh, old man had jokes.

"Dad, just the man we wanted to see." Jules gave me a what the fuck look but we both know we were gonna need dad in on this shit. We just wanted to have more to go on before bringing him. Well he's here now so what the fuck!

"Oh yeah, what're you two up to?"

"Nothing dad."

"Jules, the last time I saw you two whispering and plotting in a corner I ended up having to replace every window in the widow Dillard's house, don't bullshit me."

"Dad seriously, she had it coming the nosy heifer was always getting us in trouble, besides we were kids."

"You're full of shit Roman, that was only last year. So come now, tell me what you two did that I have to fix, and if you haven't done it yet, then don't."

"You tell him Roman."

"Pussy."

"You know it."

"Uh, so yeah, we sorta hacked into the sheriffs' computer at the station."

"You..." Dad looked like he was ready to blow.

"Dad before you blast us for that shit I think you should hear us out, because what we found might save lives."

"What the hell are you talking about Roman?"

"I think it will be better if we showed you."

I went to retrieve the papers Jules and I had hidden away.

Coming back into the room I passed them off to my father without saying anything. I wanted to see if he would see what we saw without us prompting him, maybe we were off or some shit.

"Is this...are they...are you fucking shitting me, is this what I think it is?"

"What do you think it is?" Jules was at the edge of his seat, I think I was holding my breath a little. I guess I was hoping against hope that we were wrong.

"Are they hunting fucking human beings?"

"You see it too huh."

"And this list of names, are these their sponsors or some shit? I know some of these fucks, what twisted fucking mind came up with this shit? Oh shit, Victoria-Lynn, she doesn't know about this does she?" He gave me a look of horror which was pretty much how I felt about that shit. My girl cannot deal with this bullshit I know it.

"No, I don't want to tell her about this shit until I have to. There's something else dad, I think he might've killed her mother."

Dad flew out of his chair in a rage. Yeah, that's about how the fuck I feel.

"Fucking son of a bitching asshole."

Yep, that's dad, it's how he handles stress. Usually it's funny as shit, but there's nothing funny about this situation, not with my baby caught in the middle.

"We have to call in Marcus." Dad started pacing back and forth.

"Uh...dad, you sure about that?"

"Yes, he's just what we need."

Jules and I looked at each other. Oh shit, I'd said that same shit before but it was only as a last resort.

"Uh, but dad, if we call him in people might be dead before we get any real answers. Shouldn't we find out if what we suspect is true first?" This shit was starting to scare even me now, if dad thought we needed uncle Marcus then shit.

"You have doubts about that?"

"Not really no, but dad, uncle Marcus is..."

"He'll keep me from putting a bullet in Kenneth Baldwin's fucking head myself, and you too. I don't want shit like that on your conscience."

"And uncle Marcus?"

"He doesn't have a soul. Besides he wouldn't see it as a sin, especially if they're guilty of this shit."

"I say we just turn the tables on them and hunt their asses down." Jules could be a bit of a savage.

"My wife raised wolves."

"Uh dad, you just got through saying your brother had no soul." I had to remind his ass, this was his brother we were talking about after all.

"He's a whole other breed son, don't compare. Now what the fuck are we gonna do about Vicki? She's in more danger than we thought you do realize that right."

"How so?" Now I was on the edge of my seat. I really hadn't thought of any more danger to her since she was out of his house.

"Son the drive from here to school is isolated. She and Petra take that route twice a day, who's to stop these fucks from pulling something? No we gotta get them out of there."

"Dad it's their last year of high school..."

"Yeah, or it could be their last year period if these twisted fucks get a hold of them Jules."

"What excuse will I give her? I don't want her knowing any of this shit, not yet anyway."

"Why don't we put a body on them?"

"That's not a bad idea Jules, until we come up with a good enough reason for taking them out of school. If these fucks mess with my daughters I'll blow this town to fuck." Yeah and mom raised wolves.

"Okay, I'll take care of it." Shit this thing is getting complicated, now I have to put a guard on my girl so she could go to school in peace.

"Good, I'm off to bed for one last night of peace and quiet before your uncle the alpha wolf shows up here. Now listen you two, when he gets here I don't care what he promises you, you don't do shit he says without clearing it with me first."

"Sure dad."

"I mean it Roman, you're too much like him as it is."

"You trying to call me psycho dad?" I play boxed him.

"There's no trying about it, you're both too much like him. I don't know where your mother went wrong."

Typical, when we were in trouble we were mom's all other times we were his. "Speaking of which, what do you plan on telling her?"

"Everything, you boys know I don't keep secrets from your mother."

"So you think I should tell Vicki?"

"Not yet son, but soon. Especially after we have some concrete evidence, this isn't something you can keep from her."

I knew he was right, but it broke my fucking heart just thinking about it.

The three of us split up and went to our separate floors for the night. Tinks was sleeping curled up on my side of the bed. I moved her out of the way and put her in her own bed on the floor next to her mother's side of the bed. Climbing in I drew my girl into my arms and inhaled her scent. My baby sighed and burrowed deeper into me.

"Roman." She sighed my name in her sleep; that shit made me smile as I pulled her even closer to me.

I didn't know how we were gonna deal with this shit yet, but I knew for damn sure I would do whatever it takes to keep her safe. If taking her out of school's the answer then she would just have to deal. You couldn't have a last year of high school if you were dead. I'd rather have her pissed off and alive.

"Babe." I called to her just before turning her onto her back and climbing between her thighs. She was naked under my t-short. I just slid right into her warmth and rocked her awake.

"Umm, haven't you had enough?"

"Never. I'll never have enough of you."

It was slow and sweet and dreamy, like the calm before the fucking storm.

Chapter 22

It's been a week and a half since dad called uncle Marcus; the crazy fuck was due here any day now. Apparently he was in the Middle East somewhere doing who knows what. Uncle Marcus used to work for one of those obscure government agencies where everything was top secret and on a need to know basis. Which meant we didn't know fuck about his dealings.

He'd left the government since and I quote 'those fucks don't know their heads from their asses.' So now he does freelance. All I know is that he was called the Hunter, and that he was damn good at what he did. Dad knew more than he was saying but that was to be expected. Jules and I were the same.

Dad would only say that he called the contact number and was told by a third party to expect a call in a day or two. When uncle called him back dad just told him it was about family, my future wife to be exact. He gave him the bare bones and that was that. Apparently hearing that his future niece was in need of his help was all the explanation needed to have him coming back to the mainland, he just needed to tie up some loose ends.

In the meantime, I hadn't taken Cheeks out of school. Instead we had the girls tagged to and from school, and when they had to go somewhere they were never alone. Neither of them seemed to catch on yet but it was only a matter of time I'm sure.

In the end my decision was based on the fact that she'd had a lot of changes in her life of late. She was dealing with the separation from her father rather well, but I could tell it still bothered her.

She never brought him up to me; the one time she'd tried I'd shut her down. I wasn't ready to tell her what we suspected, but I wasn't willing to watch her tear herself up over him either.

Now with Uncle Marcus coming I didn't have much of a choice, I will have to share some of what I'd learned with her.

This did not sit well with me. I'm the type of guy who doesn't think my woman needs to be burdened with bullshit, that's my job. I could give a fuck who agreed with my point of view.

She should enjoy the good things in life. Like shopping with my mom and sister, helping mom in the kitchen concocting shit that was kick ass or laughing at some silly show on TV. Worrying about her father and his sick fucking twisted ass was not part of that equation. Not to mention even thinking that there was a possibility her dad had offed her mother.

Before the whole kissing the dog thing where I had gone off the rails for a minute, I had always protected her. It was my place as her man, she was still young, still had a lot of life to live. She had enough to deal with what with high school and all the drama that came with that fuckery.

I was never your average kid, with a brain like mine it was never gonna happen; always been ahead of my peers in that way. I know my way of thinking doesn't fit the norm, but I could give a fuck. She was mine to protect. This isn't a run of the mill relationship, not something that would end when we went off to college and real life. This is our life, and will remain so for as long as we both have life in our bodies if I had anything to say about it.

So therefore how I handled sharing this information was very important, the fact that I would rather not tell her shit was still foremost in my mind.

I rolled over in bed where she was still asleep beside me. So peaceful, so beautiful and all mine. I would fucking kill for her and if that son of a bitch did anything else to her I will end him without a second thought. Asshole. His hunting games aside what I now suspected him of subjecting her to all these years was enough for me to want to tear his ass apart.

"Wake up baby."

"Hmmm?"

" I need you, wake up." Before she was fully awake I took her mouth, warm, tender, sweet. She opened to me automatically the way she always did. I drew her body closer to mine, letting her feel my need between her legs.

"Open."

She opened her already naked thighs for me. I kissed and nibbled my way down her body paying special attention to her magnificent tits. I knew they were her hot spot. I could make her cum from sucking on her nipples alone, that's how sensitive they were.

Her hands roamed over my shoulders and down my back to my ass trying to draw me into her but I kept on my path licking my way down her middle until I reached her sweet, warm pussy.

"Open baby." I helped her keep them opened wide with my hands on her knees baring her to my eyes and mouth.

I licked all around her opening, teasing her. I want to drive her crazy with my tongue before I fuck her. This won't be a rush to the finish, I felt the need to feast on her flesh, to explore, to enjoy.

Opening her with my thumbs I licked until I felt her juices start to flow into my mouth.

"Roman...please."

Fuck, her voice told me she was already far-gone and I'd only just begun. Knowing I was about to introduce something ugly into her life, I needed to share beauty with her first.

"Not yet babygirl."

I went back to sucking on her while pushing two fingers slowly into her. Her back arched as she cried out, flooding my tongue with her sweetness. My dick was hard and pulsing as it laid trapped against the bed beneath me but still I took my time.

She pulled on my hair to get my attention. I left her pussy intending to find her lips but she had other ideas.

"Fuck baby."

She pushed me to my back and attacked my cock with her hands, mouth, teeth.

She licked my crown and nibbled her way gently down my shaft before swallowing my length, her hand on my balls cupping me.

"Fuuuuuuuck." I pushed my hips up setting a fucking motion in and out of her mouth, with a tight grip on her hair I guided her head up and down. She groaned around my dick and I felt that shit in my toes. When she used her own fingers to pleasure herself plunging them in and out of her heat I finally lost it. Shit, there goes tender.

I pulled her off my dick and kissed her hard, long and deep. Then I turned her around and drove into her pussy from behind.

She was already cumming when I made the first stroke into her.

"Fuck, fuck, fuck, so fucking good baby."

I grabbed her hips and powered into her, her pussy gripped me like a fucking glove. The arch of her back; so fucking beautiful, the way she ground her ass back at me, taking all of me, the wet sounds coming from where we were joined it all combined to make me lose my fucking mind.

There was nothing slow and easy about this shit, she wouldn't let me. She dropped from her forearms letting her chest meet the bed, which only sent her ass higher into the air. I took that, as my opportunity to push my thumb into her ass and that was all it took for her to start creaming my dick again. Her spasms set me off and I flooded her pussy with my jizz.

Still connected I pulled her back to me and laid spoon fashion on the bed until we caught our breaths with me still buried inside her.

"I love you Victoria-Lynn." I kissed her hot cheek.

She reached her hand back and grabbed behind my neck.

"I love you too."

We shared one last kiss before settling down to wait for the sun to come up.

Victoria-Lynn

Something's going on with Roman, what that is I haven't a clue. I just know he's being very tight lipped and him and his dad and brother are always closed off somewhere. Whenever I'd ask he would just tell me not to worry that everything was okay, but how could I not? I had a feeling it had to do with my father; I really wish he would leave it alone. I'd learned long ago how to deal with my father's temper. Of course this last time hadn't been the first time he'd hit me. When I was younger it had been more frequent. But now either because I'd learned how to tell the signs of an impending episode or because I was out of the house more, they had lessened.

That's why Roman's behavior after the whole Timothy thing had scared me so much. I didn't need another abuser in my life, but I knew Roman was nothing like dad. Dad hit me for just being, Roman's spanking aside, I don't think he would ever fold his fist and punch me in the face. We'd talked about his anger, at night while we laid in bed planning our future and what we wanted to have together. He'd explained that what I'd done with Timothy was some kind of trigger for him, and since I had no plans on repeating that we should be okay. He did say that if he thought I needed a spanking in the future he would have no problem administering one.

Spankings were kinda fun but I wouldn't let him in on that secret. Maybe sometimes, not often mind you, I would misbehave just so I could get him all riled and heat up my ass.

ROMAN

We finally made it downstairs in time for breakfast. She'd looked so well fucked and hot in our bed that I'd had to break off another one. Then in the shower her sweet pussy, all clean and wet had begged for my tongue; what was a guy to do?

Let's just say there were two well-fucked individuals who walked downstairs hand in hand for breakfast.

The rest of the family was already gathered around the breakfast table, including Melanie who had only been back the night before. So far she was behaving herself but I didn't trust that bitch so I was keeping an eye on her ass.

Talk was lighthearted with Jules and Victoria-Lynn teasing each other about some tae bo competition they had going the day before. My girl thought she was tough shit.

"Thaddeus you fuck, what did I tell you about locking your doors moron? The human race is fucked in the head don't you get it?" This hard framed carbon copy of my dad entered the room, rounded the table and picked up my squealing mother.

"Marky you're home." She was the only one who got away with calling him that.

"Natalia darling you ready to ditch this asshole and run away with me? I know just the place." He kissed her loudly and winked at dad.

"Unhand my wife you ass, go get your own girl."

He released mom long enough to grab dad in a full on hug, no man hug for these two, they even did the kissing the cheeks thing. Fucking Italians.

Fuck, Uncle Marcus was here, I guess I had no choice but to let her in on this shit now.

Chapter 23

With my uncle here I was on tenterhooks for a good minute, hoping that he didn't say anything until I had a chance to talk to her first, but I should've known better. He acted as though he was just dropping in to check up on his family. Regaling us with tales of some of his exploits while flirting shamelessly with the women. He seemed taken with my girl, teasing her and telling mom he was throwing her over for the newest Blair bride.

I relaxed once I realized he wasn't going to just blurt shit out at the table, but I still had to tell her something. What, I still wasn't sure, but when he gave my dad, Jules and I a look I knew playtime was over.

"We men are going out back for a cigar Natalia." Dad bent to kiss mom and rub her shoulder before leaving the room. I knew he'd told her what was going on, possibly all of it. I don't know how he could, for me, the thought of worrying cheeks with this shit left a bad taste in my mouth. I guess I had a different way of thinking. Dad believed that sharing everything with your mate went a long way to keeping the peace. I believe that the man should handle the bullshit and let the woman just enjoy the good, antiquated, yes. Who gives a fuck?

How exactly was she going to handle hearing this shit? What was she going to do with the info? See what I mean, all this will do is make her scared, worried and miserable. If I just took care of it and told her after the fact when there was nothing left to worry about wouldn't that be better? Both dad and Jules seemed to think that was warped thinking, I'm still not sure.

Of course dad and uncle Marcus lit up, both Jules and I declined I just wanted to get shit started. The sooner we got the planning stage done the sooner we could get to the doing stage. I wanted this shit over and done with as soon as possible.

Vicki has been settling in to her new life here with my family and I. Her schoolwork hasn't suffered any that I could see and she was getting back to her old self again. We hadn't had an argument since she moved in which should be a good thing, but I didn't like it. It was as if she was afraid to say or do the wrong thing and I couldn't figure out if that's because she was afraid she would be asked to leave, or if it was remnants from my caveman antics when she kissed that asshole. Either way I was going to have to have a talk with her about that shit. I don't want her afraid of anything, I know I'd threatened to leave her and had in essence left her for a short time but that shit right there had taught me that

I couldn't live without her ass so there was no way I was ever leaving her again.

"We've got a problem here boys." Uncle Marcus's voice brought me back to the matter at hand. We all turned to look at him expectantly.

"I didn't just arrive, I've been here for a few days. After what you told me Thaddeus I had to do some recon, couldn't go in blind.

Now here's what I've pieced together so far. This game that the men are playing goes beyond this place, it's almost like a fucking cult. In the last few days I've been able to gather names and locations but I'm afraid it's bigger than we thought. I have a lot of work to do in the next few days, but before we get into that." At this point he turned to Jules and clasped his shoulder.

"How serious are you about that little lady in there son?" Julius got a confused look on his face, as did dad and I. What the hell was he talking about? Did he mistakenly think it was Julius's girl he was here for? I looked at dad who just shrugged his shoulders.

"I don't understand the question." Jules was still wearing a look of bafflement.

Uncle Marcus reached inside his jacket and pulled out a Manila envelope. Dropping it on the table he opened it and pulled out some stills. There were surveillance shots of Vicki and Petra at different times throughout the day. From them leaving home, some of them on their lunch break outside on school grounds and then the return home. I didn't quite understand why he needed those but what the hell. Maybe he was just really thorough. He even had their detail in some of the shots at least it showed the guy was on the job.

It was the last ten pictures that shed some light on the question though. In them Melanie could be seen meeting with Kenneth Baldwin.

"What the fuck?" My first intention was to go into the house and get Vicki away from her out of harms way, then smack the bitch in her face.

"What is that, what the fuck is that?" Jules backed away like it was a ticking time bomb about to go off in his face.

"I'm sorry son, how serious are you?"

"Don't ask me that now, what the fuck?" Jules turned to look back in the house.

"Don't look inside I don't want to show my hand just yet. The reality is I have no audio, I was just doing some groundwork before I get started, I didn't expect this little hiccup. Let's not jump to conclusions I just wanted you to know going in, okay. Moving along, as I said in the beginning, this thing is big. There're some names and faces that cropped up that...let's just say this shit is going to turn over a lot of apple carts. There're some seriously moneyed people on my list so far. You know where money is concerned there're payoffs and hush money and all that other bullshit to work through."

"I think you're forgetting brother, we have money too and that's my daughter in law in there. In the long run this is about her, her safety. I want to make sure this animal can't come after her ever. What about the other thing?"

"About that, I've been making some inquiries, kind of on the sly you know. I'm an old pen pal who lost touch and would like to reconnect. Most people I talked to seem to believe the running away story, but there were a few that I kinda got that vibe from. You know, when they think they know something but don't want to share less they're wrong. I'll focus on those. I'm thinking this hunting shit is a more direct threat at the moment. If he murdered her she's been gone for a long time, a few more weeks give or take isn't going to make a difference."

I hardly heard all of what was said after that I was too busy holding myself back from rushing into the house and getting her. My baby, the fuck!

"What do you want us to do about Melanie?"

"That's a good question Thaddeus, I was thinking leave things as is. If she's sharing info obviously we can't share anything pertinent in front of her, but we can give misleading info. On the other hand if we just cut her off suddenly she'll probably figure out something's going on and give them a heads up. How much does she know about what I do?"

"Nothing, we don't discuss your work outside the family uncle Marcus you know that."

"Alright, I just thought that since you two have been together so long you might've..."

"If we'd been married...maybe...but..." He got a pained look on his face. This had to be hard as fuck for him, realizing that his woman was nowhere near what he thought she was.

"Uncle Marcus thanks for coming, for doing all this, I gotta go, I need to get Vicki away from her I'm sorry but it's killing me."

I didn't wait for an answer just walked through the door into the room, took Vicki by the hand and walked away.

"Baby, what are you doing?" She laughed as I practically raced up the stairs dragging her behind me.

"I was talking to your mom...Roman, what is it, what's wrong?" She finally sensed the tension in my body. I was strung so tight I didn't even know what I was doing. All I know is that I needed to hold her, to protect her, stand between her and all the ugliness I knew was coming. I was going to have to tell her everything. Seeing her sitting so close to her enemy, having no idea of the danger, the threat that Melanie might pose was an eye opener for me.

It wasn't only about what dad and Jules had said, it was about us handling it together. I could still shield her but this way she would know where the danger lay.

Not now though, right now my need for her superseded everything else. The reality of what we were facing finally set in with my uncle here. What had started as a need for revenge had now blown up into something sinister, something that I knew was going to do my girl grave harm emotionally. I'd be fucked if I'd let anyone harm her physically.

One more night, I'll give her one more night before I knock her world off its axis.

Tinks was laying sprawled on her bed, damn dog had a ribbon in her hair, that was just fucking wrong.

The incongruity of my thoughts was almost funny. Here I am in the middle of this horror movie bullshit and I'm stressing about the dog wearing a ribbon.

"Roman you're beginning to worry me, what's wrong?" She clasped my face between her hands.

"Nothing's wrong babe, I just missed you that's all."

"I call bullshit." She grinned at me.

How long will that grin disappear for? That grin, the thought of it disappearing made me regret every harsh word I'd ever said to her. I actually felt a pain in my heart. Her face, fuck me, her beautiful, perfect face, those eyes looking at me with love, what had I almost done?

"I'm so fucking sorry baby." I pulled her to me, her shirt clutched tightly in my hands at her back, my face buried in her neck as I felt my fucking heart break.

He'd fucking abused her for years I had no doubt, and I'd spit in her face, oh fuck. I ran to the bathroom where I emptied my stomach. I actually hated myself in that moment. As I'm kneeling there trying to pull myself together she knelt down beside me, hand on my brow checking for fever.

"Baby are you sick?" There was a tremor of fear in her voice.

"Shh, no don't cry, I'm not sick." I cleaned myself up before leading her back into the bedroom.

"Let's just lay down together babe I wanna hold my girl."

She was still looking at me with sad worried eyes. How could I have ever fucking hurt her, doubt her? I have no doubt now that she'd been telling me the truth all along. Her home life was so fucked it was a wonder she hadn't done worse.

I laid her on top of me, her head under my chin, my arms and legs wrapped tightly around her.

"I love you baby, I'll always love you, I'm sorry I hurt you, sorry I was such a horse's ass. You forgive me?"

"Of course I forgive you, I love you remember." She petted my chest soothingly, now she was the one offering comfort when I had the strong need to do that for her.

Don't cry Blair you little bitch, fuck you I'm having a moment with my girl. My subconscious is a bigger fuck than I am.

"Roman..."

"Hmm?"

"Tell me what's wrong..."

"Nothing's wrong baby, everything's just fine. I'll tell you what we were talking about tomorrow okay, just not tonight. But I want you to know that there's nothing for you to worry about, not ever, no matter what's going on I'll protect you always. You believe me?"

"You always protect me Roman."

Yeah, except when I'm being the one you need protection from. Am I ever going to get over this now? Knowing the fucked up shit she'd been through makes what I'd done seem monstrous. Will there ever be a day when I can look at her and not remember my anger and the pain I'd caused her? I'll just have to spend the rest of my life making it up to her.

"Victoria-Lynn will you marry me?"

Chapter 24

I felt a huge sense of calm after asking her to marry me, I always knew I'd ask her some day just not this soon. Her life is about to change drastically. She'd probably feel like she had no stability since her father is a monster who apparently offed her mother and had been terrorizing her her whole life. With my ring on her finger and my last name not to mention the power of the Blair family behind her, she can't help but feel more secure. At least that's what I'm hoping for. Yes this is a good thing.

"Are you gonna answer me or what?" For the last five minutes she's been staring at me wordlessly.

"You...you want to marry me?"

"Baby what the fuck? How can you be surprised at this shit? Tell me you've always known that this is where we were headed. How could you not know? No don't cry." She was crying and clutching onto me.

Man so soft, so little, how do I always forget what a tiny thing she is?

"I thought you changed your mind after...

"Victoria-Lynn no matter how mad I get at you now, or in the future, I'll always love you. They'll never be a time when I'm not in love with you. Can you try to remember that shit for me please?"

"Yes...yes I'll marry you, I love you." She started kissing all over my face while she cried.

"Okay baby, but you gotta stop that crying shit, you know what that does to me." She sniffled and wiped her tears while I combed my fingers through her hair. I hated knowing that

I had to fucking destroy her world. I was gonna wait until in the morning but, fuck.

"I have something to tell you." Why wait? There was no point I'll tell her what was going on, answer her questions and hopefully my love and support will be enough to keep her from falling apart. I hope I was doing the right thing here though shit.

"Is it bad?" She looked up at me with a little fear.

"It doesn't matter, all that matters is that you're safe. No matter what happens hold on to that, you're safe and I love you. We have each other now and always nothing means more than that okay."

"Okay Roman." She laid her head on my chest and I took a deep breath. How much did she know or suspect about father? I had not a clue, she'd never once let on that there was anything going on. She'd hid her own abuse very well so who knows.

"How much do you remember about your mom?" I held my breath as I waited for her answer.

"My ...um...what? Not much, I was so young when she left...why?"

"Did you ever hear from her after she left? Anyone ever said they saw her?"

"No, my dad said she moved away somewhere."

"Do you remember her at all?"

"No, not really I just remember her hugging me a lot, and sometimes crying."

Her body shook and I hugged her closer.

"What?"

"I think he used to hit her. I'm not sure but when I was younger, right after she left, I kept having this recurring dream or at least I think it was a dream. She'd always be crying and holding her face. When I was old enough to ask he just told me that it was my imagination. Then as I grew older the dreams just stopped, I'd forgotten all about them. Why are you asking me about my mom?"

I blew out a breath. "We think there's a possibility that he might've killed your mother."

She jumped and tried to get out of bed but I held her tight. She covered her ears and the tears started again as she rocked back and forth in my arms. She was crying so hard there was no sound coming out of her throat. I rubbed her back soothingly until she caught her breath again.

"Talk to me baby, don't shut down." Fuck, maybe I should've waited after all.

"I think I knew, I think I always knew but I shut it out. What did he do to her?"

"We don't know yet, we're only just piecing it together and it's looking more and more like a possibility.

There's something else...it appears that your father and Stephen Crafton along with some other very prominent men in the state and elsewhere are involved in some kind of game. A game in which human beings are hunted for sport." I let the words settle in and waited.

She got away from me that time and made a run for the bathroom. I was hot on her heels as she threw up and retched. Holding her hair back was the best I could do as I watched her suffer.

She cried and gagged at the same time. I had to hold her up as her body seemed to just give out on her.

"Are you sure about this?"

"Yeah, Jules and I found out about it when we broke into his files. That's why my uncle Marcus is here, he knows more about this stuff than we do so he's here to take care of it. He's already spoken to someone who might have some information about what really happened to your mother. We believe he killed her, we just don't know how or why. And if he did, where's the body?"

"The apple tree in the backyard."

"Pardon me?"

"The apple tree in the backyard, he planted that when I was younger maybe right around the time she supposedly ran off. He told me it was to remind me of her or something like that."

It can't be that easy. I wanted to run downstairs and get the others right away. Get on it, see if we could uncover his crime so easily, but I couldn't leave her, not in this state.

"Come back to bed baby don't sit on the cold floor."

Tinks must've picked up on her mama's stress because she came galloping into the room and landed in her lap.

Victoria-Lynn tickled her and was lost in the dog's antics for a good five minutes while I watched my two girls. Picking them both up in my arms I carried them back to the bed.

Sitting with my back to the headboard, I held them between my legs and closed my arms around her enfolding her, protecting her. "If you remember anything else baby, tell me okay."

"What're you going to do? Please Roman just let the others take care of it don't get involved.

" I can't do that baby, it's my responsibility, you're my responsibility I have to be involved. I promise not to do anything stupid though okay. One more thing stay away from Melanie, uncle saw her talking to the sheriff. We don't know exactly what the hell that was about but we're gonna find out. In the meantime I know you don't really deal with her but you're gonna have to cut back on that even more. Do not be anywhere alone with her, I don't give a fuck what reason anyone else gives you don't do it you hear me?"

"Yes, I still don't understand why she hates me so much though."

"Because she's an insecure bitch who needs to be the center of attention fuck her, she doesn't matter to us and I don't want you worrying about any of this shit either."

"But if this is true, he's my dad. People are gonna know he's monster. I never wanted anyone to know, that's why I hid...for so long...oh Roman what am I going to do?"

"Victoria-Lynn, what do you mean you hid for so long, hid what?" It was one thing to suspect that her father had been hurting her and quite another for her to admit it. She'd only owned up to the slap in the face because of the glaring evidence, now this. "What did he do to you?"

"Nothing, he didn't do anything." She turned around in my arms.

"What...did...he...do?"

"I'm not telling you."

"Fuck this shit." I tried to get out from behind her but she played the human vine again. Arms and legs wrapped around me keeping me in place. Tinks thought we were playing around and started running around in circles on the bed and yipping her head off.

"Roman you can't fight everyone, stop it what he did or didn't do is in the past. I'm here aren't I? You saved me...you don't have to do anything else."

"What did he do to you cheeks?" I held her face in my hands.

"Oh Roman... sometimes he'd get upset and he'd lash out at me okay, or if he'd been drinking he'd get angry..."

"How often?"

"What?"

"How often did he hit you?"

"Not a lot." She blushed and ducked her head.

"Don't fucking lie to me."

"Do we have to do this?"

"Yes we do, now tell me what that fuck did to you."

"On average... at least once a week."

"Once a..." I jumped off the bed and headed out of the room and down the stairs.

I found dad and uncle Marcus in the den, Jules was nowhere to be found and I guess mom and Petra had gone off somewhere. Victoria-Lynn was right behind me as I walked into the room.

"I don't care what you find or don't find, I want him fucking dead."

"Son what's wrong?" Dad was up and coming towards me.

"He fucking beat her at least once a week. How could I not know this, how? Why did you keep this shit from me Victoria-Lynn?"

"Because I knew you'd react this way you're going to get into trouble, please Roman, let it go. Please, for me."

"Son calm down we'll take care of it but don't go doing anything stupid. I told you before, you end up in jail she's out here on her own, you don't want that."

"Dad, do you have any idea how this makes me feel, any idea at all what I want to do to him? Look at her really look at her. She's what five two a hundred pounds? The sheriffs over six feet tall and weighs two fifty at least and you know he didn't pull his punches." I looked at her then and walked pulled her away so the others couldn't hear.

"All those times you were too tired or whatever fucking excuse you gave me, he was beating the shit out of you and I didn't know. I was supposed to be protecting you, you didn't let me protect you, I hate that you didn't let me protect you. I'll never forgive myself for not taking better care of you."

"Roman...don't, it's not your fault."

I pulled my hair as my head threatened to explode. Dad slapped my back reassuringly.

"Nephew, no worries, what's done is done. You can't go back and change anything, that day's already gone never to be repeated. What you can do is make sure her life from now is nothing but roses, you can be the man I know you are and reassure her that you're not going to do anything stupid that'll take you away from her. You can reassure her that she's safe now and that no one will ever get to her again."

"Are you going to take him out or am I?"

"Boy didn't you hear anything I said?"

"Uncle he fucking beat the shit out of her right under my fucking nose for over a year. What would you do?

"I'd get angry yes, but I hope that if someone gave me some good advice that I'd follow it. I hope that I could put aside my anger and take care of the special lady in my life and realize that my erratic behavior is hurting more than helping."

Fuck, he called me out in front of my girl. She's standing there clutching Tinks in one hand and my shirt in the other. Even the damn dog was looking at me disapprovingly. Pulling her into my chest I held her for a while before just nodding to my dad and uncle and leading her out of the room and back up the stairs.

In the room I sat her on the bed and paced as I tried to get my thoughts together. Kneeling in front of her, I took her hands in mine as Tinks sat on her lap.

"I'm sorry I hurt you, I'm sorry that I didn't know what kind of fucked up pressure you were under. Most of all I'm sorry I added to your terror. Never again Victoria-Lynn, as long as we live I will never hurt you again, I give you my solemn oath. Don't cry baby come here." I pulled her into my arms and climbed onto the bed holding her to my heart. A heart that was so full of love for this one person it threatened to consume me completely. The pain would go away eventually I know, but the guilt will linger I was certain. One thing was for sure, I'm gonna fucking gut the sheriff.

Chapter 25

Things were hectic for the next few days, the cat was out of the bag now and Vicki knew what was going on, there was no sense in keeping anything from her. Jules was trying to find out in a roundabout way what Melanie's connection to the sheriff was without tipping her off. Personally I say beat the truth out of the scheming bitch but she's his to deal with not mine. Not yet anyway, if I find out she's done anything to hurt Victoria-Lynn it'll be her ass though. She's been steering clear of me lately because I couldn't find it in me to play nice to find out what she knows so every time her ass got too close I gave her the 'you're gonna come up missing glare.'

If she walked into a room even with others there I went and got cheeks the fuck out. I have no idea what Jules told her about my behavior and quite frankly could give a fuck. Victoria-Lynn is now my only concern. It was hell going off to the hospital and sending her off to school when there was so much to be done and things were so unstable.

Lately I've become very clingy, I hated for her to be out of my sight. And when we slept, I kept her body damn near buried under mine. How the poor girl got any sleep like that was beyond me, but she never complained, just held me as tight as I held her.

Uncle has been gathering more info in the few days he's been here. He thinks in a situation like this with so many heavy players we needed to cross all our T's and dot every I; though he says he's not above capping someone if the need arose.

Right now we're focusing on the neighbor who has information on Stephanie Baldwin's disappearance.

Dad, uncle and I are right this minute sitting in her living room. Mrs. Dillard is a lady in her early eighties who prides herself on the fact that she's lived alone for the last twenty years and is very self-reliant. She remembers the young Stephanie Baldwin as a beautiful vivacious girl who came to the neighborhood as a blushing bride and soon became a dull shell of herself.

"She was a beautiful young girl, all of eighteen when they got married I believe...That first year you couldn't ask for a better neighbor. She picked up little odds and ends from the store for me when I couldn't get out, helped me with my yard work, little things that added up you know. Then gradually things started changing..."

"Can you remember anything that was going on at the time, anything that you might attribute to the change?" We'd decided to let uncle Marcus do the questioning and we'd jump in if we thought of something he hadn't. That was probably best since I'm not sure she'd forgiven me and Jules for breaking her windows.

"Well let's see now, that was so long ago, hmm... let's see. I think that that's right about the time him and Stephen started carrying on around here. He wasn't sheriff then of course, wasn't much of a deputy either if you want to know the truth. But some body apparently put in a good word for him and he landed the job after a couple of years at the community college and then whatever training he had to put in."

"You say they started carrying on, in what way?"

"Well now, there was a lot of coming and going, that much I remember, all hours of night. A whole lot of creepy characters in their hunting trucks tearing up and down the streets, no respect for a body. Of course he was the police so what could you do?"

"Let's go back to Stephanie for a second, what do you remember about the night she disappeared?"

"Hmm, heard the baby screaming from all the way over here, she had to be three at the time then. That's what caught my notice, Stephanie never let that baby cry like that, not ever."

"What makes you so sure that she was even there, maybe she'd already left."

"No she didn't either, seen her with my own two eyes not five minutes earlier pacing back and forth in the window before his truck showed up. Don't know what all was going on over there but in the days leading up to that night there was a lot of screaming going on over there."

She dropped her voice an octave here as if afraid someone might hear her. "I think he was hitting on that poor girl. You know back then we didn't make too much of those things and people stayed to themselves, not like today.

When I think back on all the little mishaps it makes me think you know. And then later, little Victoria-Lynn became prone to accidents herself too if you know what I mean, disgusting." She shook her head sadly.

I wanted to hunt the fucker down and drive a stake through his black heart. I was sitting there with my legs shaking like I needed a fix. What I really needed was that fucker's blood on my hands. The more she talked, the more convinced I became that he'd offed his wife the fucking douche.

"What else happened that night? You heard the baby screaming and then?"

"Then nothing. But I peeped outside a little while later because it was all quiet like. I'd gotten so accustomed to the hollering back-and-forth between them that went on for hours, I guess I was a little surprised that it ended so quickly. Mind you I could never really make out the words but no one yelled like that if they were just talking. Then I saw Stephen's truck pull up outside and the two of them got some tools out the back and went around to the yard. I think they were digging something back there because they had shovels and the like. Anyway the next day I see Kenneth drive up with a young apple tree in his truck bed. Mind you Stephanie had always told me that Kenneth hated anything to do with gardening and the like. Then of course there was no Stephanie out in the front yard with little Victoria-Lynn the next day. Next I heard they were saying that she'd run off but I knew better. That girl would've never left her baby, she loved that little girl something fierce." She nodded her head emphatically.

"So what do you think happened Mrs. Dillard?"

"Well now, no one pays me to think do they, but I'll give you my opinion nonetheless. I think he did her in and buried her in the backyard under that tree."

"If you thought that why didn't you ever tell anyone?"

"Well, at first I waited for someone to come around asking questions, but after a few days of nothing I started asking around and that's when I heard that awful lie he's been telling everyone ever since. How she'd ran off with some man. What man I ask you? The girl hardly left the yard unless it was to be inside the house, he had her so afraid she hardly stopped by anymore to have a chat. I'm telling you, you don't have to take my word for it but I believe she's buried under that tree."

I felt my skin grow cold, that's the same tree Victoria-Lynn had told me about, I was sure of it. Could he really have done this? Even with everything else we've been uncovering about his sick fucking ass this was just...How the fuck did he still appear human?

"Now back then with everyone going around spreading that filth, who was I going to tell? In those days people just disappeared as I'm sure Stephanie found out, and no one came looking, not for long anyway. Next thing I know, Kenneth's the sheriff and everyone just took it as gold that she ran off and left her child. Broke my heart to see that little girl grow up believing that about her mama. She ought to have known that her mama loved her completely. Of course he never let me near her, he'd always hated my closeness with Stephanie, now I know why."

"Thanks for your time Mrs. Dillard, you've been a lot of help." We stood to leave.

"Does this mean you're going to finally do something about that poor girl?"

"Looks like. Let's just keep this little talk between us though shall we."

"I'm not stupid young man, I watch Discovery Channel. I'll tell you the world sure is a changed place, yes indeed, everybody's lost their dang blamed minds."

We started to leave her house through the back way when uncle thought of something else to ask.

"Have you seen any other suspicious activities around here in the last few years? Anything that made you uncomfortable?"

"Well..., except for the traffic back-and-forth and the strange cars, sometimes from out of town, I can't say that I have.

Then of course there were the visits from ambassador Johnston. Use to wonder what his elitist ass was doing in these parts. Mind you, all of this took place in the dead of night when any decent body was in bed. But who can sleep with all that racket?"

"Racket?" I had to ask.

"All the hooting and hollering. Seems to me those men always had something to celebrate, dang near every other weekend or there about. And always in the dead of night, and let's not get started on the empty beer cans all over the place the next day. At first I thought somebody had complained and that's why the ambassador came out, but that doesn't make much sense now does it?"

"Thanks again Mrs. Dillard we'll be seeing you." We each shook her hand as we took our leave.

"Thank you young man for giving me the opportunity to finally get this off my chest after all these years."

As soon as we were out of earshot I said what I'm sure we were all thinking.

"Fuck, ambassador Johnston, Melanie's father. What the fuck could he have to do with this shit, and what does Melanie know about it?" Give me a reason bitch, just one. I've been waiting to break her fucking neck. I'm sure if she were involved in this shit

my brother wouldn't mind. He'd
probably want to do it himself.

Chapter 26

"Obviously there's more going on here with Melanie than we know, so now we'll have to be very careful when dealing with her. I have an idea of how to handle that though, let me give it some thought. It's not the wisest thing to go up against an American ambassador unless we have all our ducks in a line, but you can bet your ass he's up to no good dealing with this bunch."

"Marcus, my son goes to these people's house, Melanie sits at the dinner table with my fucking wife, fuck them, if they're involved in this shit I want them taken care of like yesterday."

"Thaddeus, you always were a hot headed shit..."

"I'm hot headed? You shoot people for a living you dick."

They went back and forth with the insults while I sat in the backseat contemplating our next move. I didn't even look at my brother who had his eyes closed with his head leaning back on his seat.

"I say we have our own little hunting game, starring the sheriff, the ambassador and all their little demented fuck pals."

"Speaking of hot heads." Uncle Marcus turned around to glare at me while dad drove.

"I don't know how sweet little Natalia deals with you lot. Now you two calm the fuck down, these things take time and planning. We want to walk away from this shit smelling like lilies, no one should even know that we're involved at all. I've already got some things in the works. I studied those files and found a pattern; the majority of their victims were either runaways or indigents, I'm going to put someone in their path..."

"Marcus..."

"Relax Thaddeus, I'm not going to grab some innocent kid off the street and put them in the line of fire, I'll use one of my operatives. While that's being set up we need to find a way into that backyard. The easy way would be to let Vicki open a case of inquiry into her mother's disappearance. We'd have to do it in another jurisdiction though. We could use the fact that the sheriff is too close to the situation and so are his deputies, that's one option but it will take time. The other option is to coordinate everything to go down together."

"How're we going to pull that off?" I sat forward in my seat.

"Easy, the same time we call in the tip off about their little sick fuck game, we tip them off about the body in the backyard. I just need to get back there long enough with my machinery to make sure she really is there."

"I don't want Vicki involved so I guess we'll go with door number two."

"She might have to become involved at some point boy."

"No."

Don't fuck with me on this uncle Marcus you won't win. I'm going to protect her from as much of this shit as I could. If she started digging into this shit and word got back to the wrong people she would be in real danger. From the list of names we'd uncovered I knew we were dealing with some heavy hitters, these men will do anything to keep their secrets hidden.

No one knew that we'd uncovered their little game so right now the only thing we had to worry about was the sheriff and whether his losing control over her would cause him to come after her. Who knows how that fuck's head worked?

Hopefully he'd never suspect that she remembered anything about the night her mom disappeared. I still felt the need to run right to the local high school and snatch her ass and take her home until this shit was over.

"I don't want Melanie anywhere near Vicki, she can't come to the house..." Jules didn't even butt in, just kept silently calm which is never a good thing.

"She might get suspicious if you guys just stop her cold turkey..."

"I don't care, she's not coming near her again. I don't know what the fuck she's up to but I don't trust that bitch. Jules can stage a breakup or some shit or I can bury her ass in the woods, I give a fuck. But she's not coming back to the house."

"I see why you three needed me, not a rational brain cell between the lot of you. Boy you can't go around offing people, these things need to be handled with care. We can probably use

Melanie to our advantage, we just need to know her part in this mess."

"I doubt she's part of the hunting parties. I think her gong to see Kenneth had more to do with getting Vicki out of our house than anything else." Dad shook his head.

"I'm not willing to bet Vicki's life on it. Whatever her reasons she was wrong, if she comes near her again I will personally gut that bitch."

"Damn you're a vicious little shit. I better get this shit figured out before you have us all swimming in blood."

"Whatever works."

Vicki was a little preoccupied that night when we went to bed. She'd been a little off all evening but I'd waited until we were alone to bring it up. "Something on your mind babe?" She cuddled closer to me as I rubbed her back.

"No Roman, everything's fine."

Like hell. "Look at me cheeks."

I moved her head on my shoulder so I could look into her eyes, they were worried and...sad.

"What's on your mind baby? You can tell me."

"My mom, what if he...and I...if she's been there all this time Roman, I use to play under that tree, I..." She broke down in tears.

I let her cry for a little bit, to get it out of her system. But when it seemed like there was no end to her pain I had to put a stop to it. "Babe please stop, you're gonna make yourself sick, you didn't do anything wrong...please."

For the first time in my life I was at a lost, I really didn't know what to do, and that sucked because she's the single most important thing in my life and I'm helpless in the face of her sorrow. There's nothing I can do to take the pain away.

"Tell me what to do for you, please, what do you need me to do?"

"Just hold me, tight, don't let go okay."

"Never. I'll never let go."

I wrapped her up as tightly as I could without actually absorbing her into my skin. It was hard to think straight with all the stuff running around in my head. Her sadness cut deep, it made me realize that there were some things in life I cannot bear for her, some burdens it wasn't possible for me to carry, things she'd have to bear on her own and I hated it.

I hated the images in my head of her as a lost little girl whose mother had just been gone one day. A little sweetheart left at the mercy of a tyrant who made her life a living hell. I never wanted to hurt anyone as much as I wanted to hurt Kenneth Baldwin in that moment. I kissed the top of her head and squeezed her tighter.

"Babe, we can't go back, we can't change what is we can only go forward. I learned something new today, something about your mom." I felt her tense up.

"No no baby, it's something good, someone who knew her before you were born and after. This person said that you were the apple of your mom's eye. That she loved and adored you, the two of you use to play out in the front yard together and you were a happy baby.

Please hold onto that. At least now we know he lied about that, she loved you, she would've never left you baby. And I can't help but think that she wouldn't want you to beat yourself up over this. She'd want you to go on with your life and find joy and love. Everything I want to give you."

"It breaks my heart."

"I know baby, but we'll make it right I promise."

Victoria-Lynn

I didn't know who Roman had spoken to today and for some reason he wasn't saying, but with everything he was saying only one thing kept playing through my head. She was under the apple tree, I had to get her out. I owed her that much for believing all these years that she'd left me in hell. I couldn't let on to Roman what I was thinking, I know him, he'd never let me go anywhere near that house, but I had to find a way.

If my father had murdered her I was going to make sure he didn't get away with it any longer, I just have to figure out what to do.

Chapter 27

Nothing has hindered our love life thankfully. Even with all the craziness going on around us I still find it hard to keep my hands off of her even though I have been taking it easy on her lately. I know her mind has been preoccupied and since I want her focused solely on me when I take her, I've been inside her less than usual these days. I didn't plan to let that situation last for much longer though.

I needed her and she needed me, now more than ever. It's like reassurance that we're here and we're strong and together. No matter what we face we'll be doing it from a place of strength and unity. Though I wouldn't take her selfishly, I won't neglect that side of our union either. I think it's very important to keep that bond. It also means that I've been making love to her a lot more lately as opposed to fucking. It's been hell reining in my body's natural tendency to want to pound away inside her and take things nice and easy. The fire in me for her is avaricious, every touch, every sense calls for me to dominate. It's the nature of my beast, but she needs gentle right now so that's what I'm giving her.

The softness of her neck under my lips as I rock back and forth into her body, the sweetness of her wet heat clenching around me as a lift her legs higher on my back. The sweet moaning sounds she utters as I brush against her cervix with the head of my cock makes me groan in ecstasy.

There's nothing like the feeling of being inside her, sharing this oneness with her. Every time, each and every time, it made me renew my pledge to protect and love her always.

"Ride me baby."

I flipped us over so that she could take the lead. With our hands clasped together next to my head she took me all in, riding my cock like she'd been starved for it.

"More Roman."

"Fuck!"

She was using my cock to fight her demons. I know when I'm being used, when I'm just needed to serve one purpose. To make her forget, I can do that, but not this way. I took her mouth in a hard kiss while sitting up beneath her and lifting her off of me.

"Come."

I took her off the bed and laid her on the floor before driving back into her. This way I could go as far and as deep in her as she needed me to. There was no give from the hardness of the floor so she could do nothing more than take the pounding of my thrusts.

"Ahhh...Roman."

"Ssh, I know, I know." I kissed her softly, at least I tried, but I ended up biting into her sweet bottom lip.

"You're so deep in me."

"It's what you need." I pulled her legs up higher around my hips, her ass gripped tightly in my hands as I gave her as much of me as she needed to keep the fears at bay.

Victoria-Lynn

I hated deceiving him, I know when he finds out he's gong to be so upset, but I can't help it. I have to find out, I have to know. If I'm really careful nothing will go wrong, I just have to play it safe.

I know my father's routine all I have to do is cut school and be back in time for the final bell. No one will be the wiser.

I had my plan all worked out. I knew where my...Kenneth kept the garden tools in the shed. Hopefully she wasn't too far down, shit, I forgot about the tree but maybe I could dig around it somehow. I don't know, I'll see, all I know is that I have to try.

I stayed in class long enough to be marked present then pulled the severe cramps card, which got me to the nurse's office for my get out of jail free card.

I was a nervous wreck the whole way there. I had to hoof it since Roman had saddled us with a driver. He was so overprotective these days. It made me feel safe and loved the way only he could and that only added to the guilt.

It's good that I had to go by foot though because this way no one would notice a strange car parked in the area and I could cut through the woods part of the way.

I was sweaty and out of breath by the time I reached the house half an hour later. I rifled through cobwebs and old brooms and rakes among other things that I did not recall us even owning, trying to find a shovel. I finally found one buried behind a lot of storage bins and boxes. I'd been digging around the tree for a good hour when I felt someone come up behind me, with my heart in my throat I turned to confront whoever it was.

"Timothy what are you doing here?" I clutched at my throat.

"I could ask you the same thing. Where's your watchdog?"

"Not now Timothy I'm busy here." How could I hide what I was doing?

"Does he know you're here?"

"Why, what does it matter to you?"

"Just asking, I know how he hates letting you out of his sight, always afraid someone's going to come along and snatch you up."

He moved his hand to touch my hair and I felt strange. I can't say that I've ever felt strange around Timothy before but for some reason I was getting a really bad feeling in the pit of my stomach. I pulled my head away at the last minute.

"What, your friends can't touch you now Vicki? You know you were mine before you ever knew this guy."

"Timothy what the hell are you talking about? I was never yours we were friends that's all we've ever been."

"We could've been more if you'd only given me a chance. I was getting close I know I was but then you met him and everything changed, suddenly I wasn't the most important thing in your life anymore."

Was he crazy, why the hell was he talking like that? "Timothy..."

"No Vicki this was fate, my dad sent me by to drop off some stuff for Kenneth and here you are. It was meant to be now he can't ever come between us."

"What the hell are you talking about, no get your hands off of me."

I felt crippling fear when he wrapped his arm around my neck and started dragging me away towards his truck. I couldn't scream, I couldn't do anything but kick my feet. I felt darkness descending from the stranglehold he had on me as he forced me into his vehicle. I didn't exactly lose consciousness as I could feel the pavement under the speeding wheels.

My heart thundered in my chest as I thought of never seeing Roman again. Never hearing his laugh, never seeing that sexy smirk of his, that boyish playfulness he showed when we were relaxed. Never be able to run my fingers through his hair again. These thoughts propelled me from near darkness and weakness to full on rage. No way, there was no way Timothy Crafton was taking that away from me.

I reached over the seat and started choking him. The truck swerved all over the road as he tried to get my hands from around his neck. "Vicki stop it you'll kill us both."

"Stop the fucking truck, I'd rather be dead than go with you." I used my nails to score his face making him scream and release the wheel while he grabbed at his face. I bit scratched and punched him in the face and head until the truck went off the road and into the ditch. I had the door open and was off and running by the time he got out. I heard him behind me but I refused to look back. I kept running back in the direction we'd come, a stitch in my side.

Out of nowhere there was a screech of burning rubber against asphalt. I heard doors opening and someone screaming my name. It was the sweetest sound I'd ever heard followed by the best feeling once I was falling into Roman's arms.

I looked up into his beloved face. "I'm sorry, so sorry, I just needed to know."

"I've got you baby, I've got you."

Everything went black but I wasn't worried, Roman will keep me safe, he would never let anything harm me, never.

Chapter 28

Victoria-Lynn

When I came to I was still lying in the car and Roman was nowhere to be found. It didn't take me long to find him, I just followed the commotion going on not too far away on the other side of the street. It looked like his father, his brother and his uncle were all trying to pull him off of a bloody mess on the ground. I jumped out of the car and ran toward him.

"Stop it Roman, stop it." The others moved out of the way as what they were doing had no effect. Wrapping my arms around him as tightly as I could I tried to pull him away. I could feel the rage coursing

264 | JORDAN SILVER

through his body as he tried valiantly to stomp Timothy into the ground.

"Please baby, please stop, please please please."

Tears were flowing down my cheeks, my body felt tired and sore but I held on. I took one look at Timothy and recoiled in horror. He was a bloody mess literally. His face had been broken and not just his nose, his arm was laying at an odd angle from his body and he was wheezing as though breathing through liquid.

"Roman he's bleeding internally we have to get him to the hospital."

"Fuck him, let the piece a shit die right here."

"You'll go to jail."

"Listen to her Roman we can work this, let me think about this for a minute." Marcus stepped forward and clapped his hand on his shoulder. "It was an attempted abduction; it took place on the Sheriff's property, we can have that place crawling with law-enforcement in no time. This is our chance, it's a fucked up way for it to happen but it's perfect. What was Crafton doing there anyway do you know Vicki?"

"He said his father sent him to drop something off for Kenneth."

"Wonder what that was, we'll check his truck. Let's call an ambulance, I'll put in a secure call to someone in the state police; tell them of the sheriff's involvement and Victoria-Lynn's suspicions. We'll embellish the truth a little to get this rolling but the secret's out now, Crafton already saw her there, there's no going back."

"I'm sorry I caused so much trouble but I had to find her. I don't want her under there another minute. Please can't we get her out?" Roman still wasn't saying anything at this point but at least he'd stopped destroying Timothy. I almost felt sorry for him; obviously my old friend had mental issues, I mean why else would he do this?

"Roman?" I shook him a little from behind but still he was lost in that place that he goes to when he gets like this. It might be a while before he comes down from his mad.

"We understand Victoria-Lynn, if she was our mother we would've probably done the same, we're just upset that you were almost hurt. Son you good now?" Thaddeus tried talking to him but still nothing. Jules came back over from somewhere. He put a jacket over my shoulder. I guess he'd gone back to the car, I hadn't even realized my clothes were torn.

"I say we use this to move; uncle can't your guy in the state police make something happen so we can get whatever warrants we need to dig up the backyard? How far did you get Vicki?"

"Not far Julius, Timothy came along before I could..." I broke off when I felt Roman tense up under my arms.

"That's where I'm headed Jules, we'll figure out the rest later but I believe all the chips will fall into place if we do this now. Let's get this guy off the streets we don't want to call too much attention to ourselves. The sheriff isn't due home for a few hours at least isn't that right Victoria-Lynn? That's why you thought it was a good time to make your move?"

I could only nod my head. All my concentration was on Roman who was beginning to scare me because I seriously believed he was weighing the pros and cons of killing Timothy. Uncle Marcus walked off to make his phone calls while Jules and Thaddeus moved in closer to us. All this while Timothy is lying comatose on the ground he's not even moving and my heart is racing out of my chest hoping the idiot doesn't die by Roman's hand.

"Come on little brother let it go. You need to take care of Vicki man, she's still shaken and she really doesn't need to be seeing this shit right now on top of everything else, come." Julius tried pulling him away but he was not moving.

"Please Roman listen to him, nothing will come from you killing him. They'd win in the end, I'd be all alone and your life will be ruined and for what? He's not worth it baby, we're worth fighting for, please just let this go, you're hurting me."

I had to use that last part because I knew even after all we'd been through in the past few months Roman never wanted to hurt me. I've come to understand that I'm his Achilles heel. That's why it's so hard for me to accept that this was all my fault. But I'll have to deal with my own stupidity later, right now I had to get my guy out of the killing rage that had a tight grip on him. I stood on my toes so I could reach his ear. What I had to say was for his ears only; I could see his family watching as I soothed the wild beast.

"We're supposed to get married and have lots of babies remember? Can't you see them now, running around in that big old house driving everyone insane? Petra will spoil the girls rotten and Julius will teach the boys all his dirty habits. We'll have a hard time getting them to ourselves because grandma Natalia would hog them every chance she gets."

I painted a picture of our future for him. The future we'd discussed many times, the life we both wanted for each other, together. He took a deep breath and his body deflated as if all the anger had just left. I was pulled around in front of him so fast I almost stumbled but he held me close and firm.

"Do it and do it quick before I finish him off." I took that opportunity to push him back and out of temptation's way. Thaddeus bent down to check Timothy's vital signs as Roman folded his fist and looked on.

"I don't feel well can you take me back to the car?" I thought it prudent to get him away from here as fast as I could because whatever leniency he had in him was hanging on by a thread. I had no doubt that Timothy's life was in danger at this very moment.

"Shit baby sorry, I didn't think; let me see, let me look at you." I didn't think it was such a good idea for him to see any scrapes and bruises I might've received during my little skirmish so I deflected his attention.

"You can do that later, please can you just hold me? I'm feeling kinda shaky." He picked me up and headed for the car, my head on his shoulder.

"Thanks for saving me Roman, I knew you would come. I didn't know how, but I knew you would not let anything happen to me." His answer was to squeeze me but he was still not saying much; that's okay at least he wasn't in a killing rage anymore.

True to his word uncle Marcus had the place crawling with law enforcement before long. We'd driven back to my old home. Timothy had been taken to the hospital under police escort; when he awakened he'd be charged with attempted abduction, which carried a stiff penalty in this state. I'd had to give a brief statement but uncle worked it out so I didn't have to go down to the station until later since I wanted to be there when and if they dug up my mother.

The old lady from across the street came over and stood on the sidewalk to watch. A look of sadness on her face as the men dug up the backyard. Roman had insisted on helping the men dig for her. I know he wanted to be the one who found her for me. I walked over to Mrs. Dillard and just stood watching, my heart heavy as men went about the business of searching for my mother's body. I couldn't bring myself to think of the many times I'd played back here as a child not knowing that I was trampling on my mother's grave.

"I'm so sorry Victoria-Lynn I think I failed you, you and your mom." I looked down at her.
"What do you mean?"
"I always suspected, when the rumors first started I always knew they weren't true but I was too sacred, too afraid of him and his power to come forward. Now I wish I had, wish I could spare you this. She wouldn't have wanted this for you; it burned me up the way the people around here just accepted that story when most should've known better. She was a sweetheart your mama was, and she loved you with everything that was in her, I know, saw it with my own two eyes. You were her everything; it might be a little late but I wanted you to know that."
And with that she turned and walked away.

"Stop."

That was Roman's voice. I turned back from watching her cross the street, tears blinding me, to see him kneel down and peer into the hole they'd dug. His head came up and our eyes connected and I knew. My knees buckled and I cried out as I fell to the ground. He was there almost before the sound escaped a second time.

"I've got you baby, I've got you." We sat there on that ground, him rocking me back and forth in his arms as people milled about around us. Natalia showed up at some point and tried to take me away from Roman but he just told her firmly and with one word "No!" and I stayed locked in his arms as I cried for my mother.

Chapter 29

ROMAN

Everything was crazy after that; sheriff Baldwin showed up and was throwing out threats against everyone while swearing that he knew nothing about the body being removed from the hole in his backyard. I wanted to punch the fucker in the face but cheeks, even as distraught as she was caught on and kept a death grip on me.

Whatever uncle had done with his call to the state police they'd done a good job of quarantining things so to speak. Because of the other aspects of the case we needed to keep things contained so that the others involved wouldn't be made aware. Uncle had left soon after the troopers had shown up, something about synchronizing his team. I hadn't even known that he'd called anyone in as yet. I know he talked about it but damn he moves fast.

There was a team of crime scene techs combing the area around the hole and the uprooted tree. The body had been wrapped in some kind of burlap sack and the men were handling it delicately while I held my girl to keep her from moving forward and contaminating the evidence.

I couldn't stop her from crying and I wouldn't even try. She hadn't even spared her father a glance, not even when he started blaming her for what was taking place. I wasn't too concerned with his shit anymore since no one else was listening to his crap. That was evident by the cuffs that were placed on his ass before he was dragged away kicking and screaming. I wonder how he'd missed the official cars and vans lining the street? You'd think the jackass might at least make a run for it. I guess he was hoping for some serious help from his sick fuck friends. I couldn't think about that now either, my mind was more on her and what was going on inside of her. She hadn't said anything after her collapse just a keening moan that had pierced my soul.

Now she just sat on my lap clutching me tight as her eyes stayed glued to the burlap sack on the grass. "What are you thinking baby? Talk to me." I kissed her hair and hugged her even closer. My only wish, that the events of this day didn't set her back. I could do a lot of things for my girl. I had the money to give her anything her heart desired, but I couldn't give her the thing I was sure she wanted most at this moment. Her mother.

I'd prepared myself for this or at least I'd told myself I had but the reality was something else entirely. If I could spare her this there's no question that I would but I was afraid there was even more heartache to come. There was still the whole hunting of humans thing to deal with, then the case of murder against her father. What was it going to do to her to have to go through that?

"Baby let me take you home." I kissed her temple needing contact with her in the worst way.

"I can't Roman; I have to go with her where're they going to take her?"

"I don't know but I'll find out stay here okay." I beckoned mom over to come stay with her while I went to take care of that.

I think I already knew that there was no way that she would be able to see her mom; not yet anyway, but I had to at least try. I left her with dad and approached the guy who was in charge. Dad and Jules were talking to some of the crime scene techs I guess they were getting the ins and outs of what was going to happen next.

"Excuse me, I was wondering if you could tell me what happens next.

My girl would like to go with her mother if you could tell us where you'll be taking her."

"You're Marcus's nephew, the younger one right?"

"Yes Roman Blair." I shook his hand.

"Bad business all-around it's going to be a fucking mess, case like this going back all these years." He shook his head and looked around at the hole and then the body. "I guess they'll be taking her to the coroner; have to determine cause of death if such a thing is still possible after all this time, we'll see. Her body is going to be treated as a crime scene for the time being though son so your girl isn't going to be able to see her maybe not for sometime. Besides it may not be a good idea for her to see her in this condition you know what I mean?"

I knew he was right but thought at least she'd know it wasn't just me telling her no. I'm thinking seriously of letting dad give her something to put her to sleep for the rest of the day, because if I was having such a hard time dealing with this shit I could only imagine what she was going through.

I had no idea this day was going to end this way, no idea she would get it into her head to do this, to come here. How the fuck had we ended up here? How had we gone from a happy go lucky couple to dealing with murder and human hunting and bullshit? How the fuck do I bring her back from this? I walked back to where she sat cuddled in mom's arms. "Mom I need a favor." We were going to be here for a while I'm sure, and I wouldn't dare ask her to leave again. If she wanted to stay until her mother was taken care of completely then that's what we'll do. Mom left to go do what I asked and returned fifteen minutes later with Tinkerbell. I saw the first sign of life in my girl's eyes since I'd helped dig her mother out of that hole.

Hours later after the team had done all they could for now we were headed home. Vicki was way too fucking quiet for me and I was beginning to worry that it was all too much for her. It was dark out by the time we left. Jules and dad had to take the lead because I could do nothing but concentrate on her and her needs. Petra had been brought to the scene after school and since her and mom refused to leave Vicki the whole family had been pretty much staked out at the scene. Uncle had called dad with an update but I still don't know what was said I really didn't care anymore. I just wanted to take care of her and say fuck everything else.

Now that I had time to think clearly my gut clenched in fear at what could've happened to her today. With all the other shit going on I'd forgotten how this all started. How I'd sensed her movements while we were at the house discussing what we should do next. Right before the phone rang and her detail had reported her skipping school. I'd told him to follow her of course but I had no doubts as to where she'd been headed. I would've done the same had it been my mom. She'd lost him when she cut through the woods but I still had a bead on her. The others had followed me out the door when I went flying out of them. The thought of her in those fucking woods almost brought me to my knees.

Then seeing her running down the street with that asshole behind her. I'm gonna have to get something with eyes because her tracker only shows movement it didn't show me the danger she was in. That's the first fucking thing I'm doing as soon as we get this shit settled. Some nut somewhere must've come up with some shit that would do what I want, otherwise I'll make the shit myself.

I couldn't very well yell at her after the fucked up day she'd had but I so wanted to tan her ass for pulling that shit. What would've happened if I hadn't put that shit in her necklace? And to think I'd felt like a heel for placing it there, thought I was invading her privacy. Well fuck that, after this she'd be lucky if I ever let her out of my sight again.

She was nodding off in my arms when dad turned to us. "How's she doing son?" I glared at him. How the fuck did he think she was doing? He actually grinned and turned back around. I looked down at her little tear stained face. My poor baby had been through it. That idea to have dad knock her out was sounding better and better. But she'll still awaken to the same fucking nightmare and it had only just begun.

When we got to the estate I had to help her out of the jeep, she had no strength left. "Lean on me baby I've got you.

When we reached the door there was a loud cracking sound and dad was screaming for everyone to get down. I didn't know what the fuck was going on until the sound echoed again and I realized someone was shooting at us. I covered Victoria-Lynn with my body as Tinkerbell started barking in fright. Dad and Jules covered mom and Petra and we crawled towards safety.

Soon there was a barrage of firepower coming from our side. Uncle Marcus and whoever was with him was retuning fire. Fuck this shit.

We got the girls inside and I headed for dad's gun case. Both mom and Vicki moved to stop me from leaving the house again but I'd passed my fucking limit; enough was fucking enough. I'd started this shit with my digging into the sheriff's business well I'm going to end it. Whoever was out there it was going to end tonight.

I ran up the stairs to my room on the other side of the house away from where I could still hear gunfire going off. Mom and Vicki were screaming after me while dad and Jules held them back. They knew not to even try stopping me my dad and brother. I'd had enough, first that fuck had put his hands on my girl and now this shit. They knew I wouldn't be satisfied just waiting for someone else to handle shit and they trusted me to be careful.

I climbed through my window and down the tree that grew there. Staying close to the ground and deep in the shadows I went around in a half circle headed in the direction the firing was coming from. I knew this place like the back of my hand, had been combing through the woods that surrounded our property since childhood, so I had a fairly good sense of where the fucker was hiding.

There was a lone gunman laying on the ground sniper fashion with his gun and scope set in the direction of my house. The woods here were thick and I knew if I moved wrong, stepped on a twig or some shit I could give myself away. I had a choice to make here did I want to maim or kill? Was I ready to take a life, and if I let this person live will they always pose a threat to us? I had no idea who the person was and I just realized my uncle might have no idea that I was out here. Had dad been able to reach him and tell him that I'd come after the shooter?

The culprit took the decision out of my hands when he prepared to shoot again. Without giving myself much time to think I just pulled up and pulled the trigger. One shot to the gun arm, I'd let whoever it was live for now. I ran forward as whoever it was howled in pain. I yelled down to my uncle to ceasefire as I kicked the fucker in the side before rolling them over.

I can't say I was expecting to be staring into the eyes of the person lying on the ground beneath me.

"Well fuck, this just keeps getting better and better."

Chapter 30

"I'm coming down and I'm bringing your would be shooter with me." I yelled down to my uncle and his team.

"Let's go you fuck." I had no mercy as I dragged my quarry by the shirt collar as the culprit cussed a blue streak; no doubt the gunshot wound in the arm was causing unbearable pain but I'd be damned if I gave fuck.

Uncle Marcus met me halfway as someone in the house turned on all the outside lights.

"You've got to be fucking kidding me." That was uncle's exclamation when he caught sight of the captive I was busy dragging through the mud and brush. He quickly walked away with his phone to his ear after that. I guess there was gonna be even more bullshit involved now.

"Man you've really fucked up royally this time." That little tidbit was offered by one of the three men dressed in special ops gear who surrounded my uncle. These guys looked like they were heading into Kabul and not a little town in Oregon. What the fuck was the world coming to? Had everyone gone fucking insane?

What the fuck was going on in this town anyway? We've got the small town sheriff murdering his young wife and spending the next fifteen years or so abusing his only child, and just for kicks on the weekends him and his sick fuck friends hunted humans for sport.

I heard the others approaching from the house, I'd almost forgotten they were there. I should be inside tending to my girl who'd been dealt shock after shock today but instead I had to be out here dealing with this bullshit. I shook the asshole in my hands just on principle. "What the fuck are you on asshole?" I couldn't think of any other reason for a rational human being to be into this shit.

"Ambassador Johnston?"

Fuck, Julius. I'd forgotten that part of this fucked up equation. This shit promised to get a hell of a lot worst before it got better. My brother was in a fucked up position no two ways about it. He'd been with that bitch for years now, almost ready to pop the question. I know this is gonna hit him hard when the dust settled and he had time to think. That makes two innocent people who were fucked over this bullshit.

"Let's move this inside who knows who else he has out there." Uncle Marcus yelled across at us still on the phone as his men moved in to take the ambassador off my hands.

"I came alone."

"Yeah, we'll take your word for it asshole." It just dawned on me that he'd shot at us while Vicki was there. Like digging up her mother who her fuck of a father had murdered in cold blood wasn't bad enough, or being almost abducted and heaven knows what else by that piece a shit Crafton this fuck had taken shots at her.

"Who were you shooting at?" I tightened my hold on him ready to fucking end him; enough of this shit.

"Garret get my nephew out of there." My uncle ordered one of his men as they reached us.

"You might not want to do that bro I'm not in the mood to be manhandled. He had the good sense to back the fuck off. "Now answer me you fuck were you shooting at her?" I shook him like a dog on a leash; the front door opened and Vicki came running out.

"Get back inside baby." She kept coming; of course I knew she would hardheaded fuck.

"Roman let him go." Her voice was scratchy from crying and I closed my eyes seeking control.

"Were you shooting at her?"

"Nephew...."

"Answer me you fuck."

"Roman no." She grabbed the arm I'd raised and held on tight.

"Look at me Roman, don't do this, look at me. Let them handle it please; I need you, please come back inside please, I'm scared."

I closed my eyes trying to shut out the sight of her hurt and scared. The sound of her cries when we dug her mother out of the ground and beneath it all was my own guilt. Will I ever get away from it?

"If you fuck with her in anyway your daughter is dead, if that's not enough I'll do your fucking wife ear to ear and sit in a fucking jail cell for the rest of my life. This ends here, you better use whatever power you have to make sure your sick fucking friends never even think about coming after her." He cringed and moaned as I squeezed the hand with the bullet in it.

I pushed back the rage, dropped the offal that I'd been about to waste my freedom over and instead grabbed hold of my lifeline. "I love you Victoria-Lynn, I'm sorry. I love you."

Uncle Marcus and his cohorts dragged the complaining Ambassador off somewhere, while Vicki pulled me towards the house. Tinkerbell came running to meet us as soon we hit the door and the distraction actually worked to bring me out of my fog. My family all stood around watching us as if they expected me to lose it again but I didn't have anything left. The day had literally taken everything out of me and I knew that if I was feeling this way that my girl was going through her own personal hell.

"I'm cool guys I'm just gonna take Vicki up for the rest of the night, I'll see you guys in the A.M."

"Sure son you two get some rest it's been a long day." Both mom and dad came over to hug her while I gave Julius a pound before grabbing my girl and my dog and heading to our rooms. I'll deal with my brother later see where his head was at. I led her straight to the shower to wash off the grime of the day.

"What the fuck?" I scared her with my outburst and she jumped. "Roman?"

"He fucking choked you?" I was now seeing the damage done to her by that asshole. There was a bruise around her neck and scratches. No wonder she'd kept that jacket tight around her neck all fucking night. I was trying to figure out how I could get to him now. I'm sure uncle had him surrounded in the hospital but there had to be a way.

"Roman I'm fine I promise." She held my face in her hands and kissed me before turning on the water. I took a cloth and bathed her black and blue throat as I felt new rage inside. She stood still and let me tend to her as gently as I could. When I was done I just drew her in and held us both under the warm water. If only it were this easy to wash this shit away.

I took her out and wiped her off before pulling one of my old t-shirts over her head and leading her to the bed. Crawling in behind her I pulled her into my arms and held her against my heart. "Shit baby you haven't eaten all day are you hungry?" she shook her head no, which was no less than I expected. I'm gonna have to watch her and make sure she takes care of herself.

"Go to sleep baby I'll watch over you."

"Will they know what he did to her?" Fuck.

"I'm not sure baby but they're gonna do their best. We'll do everything we can for her now I promise." She didn't say anything else for the longest time and I thought maybe she'd fallen asleep. I kissed her head and settled down prepared to stay awake in case she needed me. It wasn't long before we were both asleep.

I kept watching her out the side of my eye to gauge exactly where she was at when we woke up the next morning. There was still residue from her tears and a hitched breath here and there that tore at my heart.

"Come here baby."

I drew her down onto my lap at the edge of the bed. Her head came down to rest under my chin and I was reminded once more of just how small she was compared to me. So small to be burdened with so much; I wondered when and how this would all end? How much would we either grow or lose from this? Will she bear the scars for the rest of her life, what?

"Roman?"

"Yes baby."

"Can you...?"

"Can I what love?" I ran my hand up and down her back soothingly. She seemed so lost.

Instead of an answer she turned in my arms to look at me, I thought she was about to ask me for something I couldn't give her like taking her back to the scene. I was going to have a hard time keeping her away from there I was sure, but I didn't want her going there everyday, feeding the guilt that had been plaguing her. But how do you help someone to move on from something that happened almost fifteen years ago when the pain was so new? She will be mourning her mom for....

Her mouth covered mine and startled me back to reality. Shit, my heart tripped over itself in my chest. What the hell was I supposed to do here? If I made love to her I'd be a selfish prick wouldn't I? I mean I always want her, no matter what's going on I want her, but she's been so hurt. Then again if I deny her she might see it as rejection. Fuck.

Her little tongue played peekaboo with mine and I went with my natural instinct and followed it with my own. She pressed her ass down on my cock, that didn't seem to have heard the conversation that was going on in my head. In the end I decided to let her take the lead, let her take what she needed from me.

Tinks slunk away into the other room, to her bed probably. She was used to her parents getting frisky a lot so she knew the deal. As her mouth and her body moved against mine I realized that I was afraid. For the first time in my life I knew gut wrenching fear and it was all for her. Is this what she really wanted right now? How will she feel after? Will there be guilt?

Taking her by the hips I moved us up and over on the bed so we could lie facing each other. With one hand around her shoulders and the other moving slowly along her side and middle I set out to soothe. That sickening feeling eased the more we kissed and I soon relaxed enough to enjoy one of my greatest pleasures, having her close to me. Feeling her heart beat in time with mine, pressing my stiff cock into her harder I tested the waters a little by turning her a little more onto her back.

"Babe are you sure?"

"Please Roman?"

Did she have to look at me like that? With those sad eyes and trembling lips? I couldn't refuse her anything, not even this. With my thumb I wiped away the tears that had fallen before lifting her head up to meet mine. I was slow and methodical as I removed first her clothes and then mine in between sharing feverish kisses.

Now instead of fighting the feeling I wanted to show her through touch just how much she was loved and will be loved for the rest of her life.

Starting at her forehead I placed soft butterfly kisses down to her cheeks, her ears, everywhere I could reach. I amazed myself at how much control I had; at how easy it was to let her needs be met first without thought to my own.

When I reached her breasts I held them close together so I could take both nipples into my mouth at once. She liked that. Her body's arching and that deep moan was evidence of that. Her tiny hand came down and took my rod in hand so she could play with it. With each stroke of her tight fist I sucked a little harder on her nipples. I could feel her wetness rubbing against me as she moved against my thigh seeking friction to ease her growing ache.

Not yet, I wanted to pay homage to her, to the beautiful girl who owned my heart. With that thought in mind I made my way down her body nibbling and sucking until I laid between her thighs. She was already swollen and pink and so fucking beautiful she made me ache. I licked her sweet pussy just to get that first taste out of the way and she spread her legs wider apart and grabbed onto my hair. That was my cue that the coast was clear. I ignored the hard throbbing of my cock as it begged me to start fucking.

With her ass in my palms I ate her pussy until she pleaded with me to stop, to end her torment; to come into her.

Her soft pleas soon became demanding cries as I dug my tongue even deeper into her while playing around her ass with the tip of one finger. I didn't penetrate her ass yet just a slight teasing with the tip the way I knew she liked. It proved to be too much for her because she soon flooded my mouth with her sweet nectar.

"Now now, now..."

She pulled my hair to get my attention so I left off enjoying the sweet taste of her juices to climb back up her body.

"Tell me what you want baby." I pressed the hardness of my cock against her wet pussy letting her feel my need for her.

"You, I want you." She reached up and pulled my mouth down to hers sucking her own essence from my tongue as I led my cock into her with my hand. When I was all in I held still for the barest of seconds before giving her what she wanted. I kept a tight rein on my own lust; fighting not to give in to the need to thrust harder, go deeper. This was about her after all, and she needed her man to be soft and caring at a time like this. I rose up on my elbows so I could look down into her eyes as I stroked in and out of her while holding her precious face in my hands.

"Is this what you wanted?" I went deep and ground my hips into hers letting her feel what she did to me even in times of turmoil.

"Yes more...please Roman I need more."

She wrapped her legs around my back opening herself even farther to me. Her grip on my cock intensified as she sucked at me with her inner muscles trying to draw the cum out of me before I was ready. I bit down on her neck and she squeezed me inside her as her juices flowed once more warming my cock until all I wanted was to stay in her forever.

Her sharp nails dug into me next but still I didn't speed up, instead I took her lips once more as I felt myself getting close. She moved faster beneath me as her cries rang out and I finally lost it, emptying myself into her while she cried. This time they tears of pleasure.

"Look at me baby." Se opened her eyes at the sound of my voice. Her eyes having lost some of their sadness were bright and questioning.

"I love you...always."

She smiled and pulled my head down.

"And I you Roman, always."

Chapter 31

The next few days were chaotic. I wasn't quite sure what had been done to the ambassador. Uncle Marcus just kept shaking his head no with a 'later' each time I even looked like I was about to broach the subject, so I left it alone for now and concentrated on my girl. There was a lot of shit to do in a murder investigation. Add the fact that it was a crime that had been committed almost fifteen years ago and the main suspect was a law enforcement officer and you had a shit storm. I knew now that my dream of keeping her out of it was just that, a dream. I did draw the line at asshole investigators who seemed to be missing the common sense gene though.

"Are you fuck stupid or is this some text book routine? How the fuck is she supposed to remember something that happened when she was a baby? Something she didn't even know had happened until a few days ago?"

"Roman..."

"No baby this is bullshit. Look you've asked her the same questions over and over again for the past half hour. She keeps telling you she doesn't know move the fuck on or get the fuck out."

"Sir it's my job to try to ferret out every kernel of memory..."

"Yeah? Well it's my job to see she doesn't get any more traumatized by this shit than she already is. She's not the criminal here go grill the fucker you have in the county lockup or wherever the fuck he is. Go to the people in the neighborhood who might actually know something. She just dug her mother out the ground what the fuck?" Vicki for some strange reason was looking at me like she wanted to laugh.

"What?"

"You're nuts. Go ahead detective, but as my fiancée so eloquently put it I don't really know much of anything. I can barely remember that night, the night she left and..." She started to shake and that was it for me.

"That's it get the fuck out."

Somewhere in the recesses of my mind I knew I was being irrational but I couldn't help it. I didn't really give a fuck what they did at this late date they should've done something about his murdering ass years ago. There wasn't much she could get from this now was there? The detective to say the least wasn't too happy with my attitude and I wasn't too torn up about it. As long as he left her alone I could give a fuck.

Mom was making funeral arrangements for as soon as the remains were released and who knew when the fuck that was going to be. My problem was getting Victoria-Lynn through the rest of this without her losing her shit. Crafton was still in the hospital and I was waiting for one of those fucks to come questioning me about why he was half dead, but uncle said not to worry he'd taken care of it. Shit if I knew he was taking care of that shit I would've ended the fuck.

There were still a lot of loose ends, like Stephen Crafton and his part in this whole sordid mess. So I asked uncle what the hell was being done after the jackass detective had left.

"Crafton's been picked up. There was no way to keep all of this out of the public so yeah. They still don't know that we know about the hunting game and we're keeping the ambassador on ice until we're ready to move forward with that."

"So what's he been picked up for?"

"His part in the cover up of the murder. My people are going through his place as we speak trying to find any evidence and any other names that we haven't been aware of as yet. This shit is gonna take a long time to clean up guys."

He looked around the table at my family who was gathered there all in support of my girl. Mom had ahold of her hand while she sat snuggled in my lap with her head on my chest. I don't even want to know what kind of fuckery was going on in her head right now listening to this sick shit.

"We've found the names of some of the victims..."

He looked at Vicki when he said this and I felt her flinch at the word victims. I gave her a squeeze and a kiss on her head. She'd argued with me to be allowed to sit in on this. I didn't want her anywhere near it but she'd insisted and against my better judgment I'd given in. I tried to remember how this had all started. Was it that kiss? I couldn't even remember anymore I just wanted it to be over so we could move on.

"Like I was saying we found some names they kept very good records which is a big help. This thing goes back many many years, so not only do we have to go searching for bodies, we also have to contact their family members and give them some closure at least. Nephew I know your main concern is your girl and getting to the bottom of what happened to her mom so I pulled some strings to get the ball rolling there. Sometimes they can drag this shit out, especially with it being a cold case. We should have something in the next couple days at least. Now as for Melanie Johnston it looks like she just made some very poor decisions in her bid to protect her father. We're not sure yet when she found out what he's been up to, but she was just trying to keep his part in all this from getting out. That's why she was so against Vicki in the first place, it was a case of too close for comfort I guess."

I looked at Jules who had his head down. At least we knew she wasn't a complete monster though I still wasn't forgiving her for the shit she did to my girl. I don't give a fuck who she was trying to protect, but for Jules's sake I'm glad the crazy bitch was just crazy and not bone deep evil.

Uncle rattled off all the shit they had to do, which truth be told I didn't really care about. Mom and dad asked all the questions and got all the answers while I kept my gaze locked on Victoria-Lynn for any sign of distress. My burning desire right now was to take her away from all this until it all blew over. But I knew she wouldn't be happy with that, not until we'd at least given her mom a proper burial. Uncle reached down to the bag that had been sitting at his feet and came back up with a handful of what looked like journals and a picture album.

"Here Vicki, we found these, looks like they were your mom's." I felt the jolt that went through her and reached for them.

"I'll take them." She was shaking harder now and I know mom felt it too because she stood up and wrapped her arms around both of us.

"You don't have to go through them now Vicki, you take your time and do it when you're ready."

She spoke soothingly to her as she held on to us. Dad's face looked like he was about to kill someone and Jules and Petra looked lost. No one really knew what the fuck to do.

"Okay that's enough for now I gotta get back anyway. By the way, the kid in the hospital is gonna live." Yeah I give a fuck.

"He's been charged with assault and attempted kidnapping which carries a pretty hefty sentence, so I don't think we have to worry too much about him. I have to go see who else was involved in this hunting shit so we can charge these fucks with this shit."

"What about the ambassador what's going to happen to him?"

Jules sounded old and tired and that fucked with me too many people were being hurt by this shit. I wondered what would've happened had I not lost my shit over that kiss? Had her father not hit her; how long would this shit have gone on and how long would she have lived her life believing the mother that had loved her had deserted her?

"Oh the ambassador's done no question but we have to play it smart. He has connections and the way I see it if he was involved there's no reason not to suspect that others of his ilk weren't. That's what we're trying to figure out now, just how high this thing went. Only the very wealthy could come up with this sick shit and apparently the others were paid very well. I'm arranging to have whatever funds we find given to the families, plus I'm pretty sure they might sue these people or their estates which I will be sure to encourage."

"I think you should go see Melanie Jules."

Shit it burnt a hole in my tongue to say that shit but if it would stop him from looking like death warmed over then whatever. He shook his head no.

"No, I understand her trying to protect her father obviously, but not like this and not over something like that. He's fucking sick, why would she try to protect that shit? That's taking loyalty a bit too far, so thanks for the offer bro but no way."

Thank fuck, I wasn't looking forward to seeing her again either and I sure the fuck wasn't too jazzed about having her around my baby. But Jules was starting to look a little rough there. Tinkerbell started bitching from up the stairs and her mama picked her head up and got up off my lap to go get her.

I worked the kinks out and was getting up to head to the kitchen for some refreshments when see came back into the room dog in hand and walked to my mom, who hugged her close. My girl needed some mom time. Not for the first time I was grateful that my parents were the fuck awesome people they are.

Epilogue

Six months later…

Well things have started to settle down around here finally, at least that's what I'd begun to think until my new wife hit me with a surprise this morning. We'd celebrated both her birthday and our nuptials in the months following the bullshit. I saw no point in waiting to tie her to me completely and though mom had a fit about the missed gala she would've loved to throw I was firm. She was now mine for always.

Her father's trial hadn't been as harrowing as we'd thought it would be. It wasn't too hard to prove that he'd done the deed and by the time the town's people had come forward, many who had kept their silence all these years in fear of retribution from the asshole, it wasn't too hard to piece the shit together. What had really cinched it though was the diary uncle Marcus had given to cheeks. Her mother had written of her suspicions that her husband and his friends might be involved in something criminal. She had believed it was drugs at first; but who knows what she'd learned in the days leading up to her murder that caused the monster to end her? She'd been smart enough to name names of the men she saw coming and going at all hours of the night. She'd even kept dates.

I went to every court hearing and so did my family when they could. We all surrounded her both physically and emotionally so she never broke. I made sure to keep myself between her and his hateful glares after the first day when I felt her tremble under his stare. "He can't touch you baby no need to be afraid." I never let go of her hand as we sat through days of testimony. By the time it was determined that he was guilty she was drained and just plain done. Contrary to what the trooper had told me that day it hadn't taken the coroner long to figure out cause of death after all. The hole in the side of Stephanie Baldwin's head was a dead giveaway. His ass was sent away forever and a fucking day. I wish they'd given his ass the chair but uncle convinced me that this was best. A few whispers in lock-up of an ex sheriff in the midst should make the rest of his existence as horrible as he'd made hers. I could live with that.

The hunting game fuckery was another matter altogether. That shit would be going on for a while, according to uncle. But thank heavens our part in it was at an end. There had been enough evidence to point the finger at the guilty. Between Stephanie Baldwin's meticulous records and dates the shit fell like a house of cards. The problem was that the network stretched way beyond Goldenlakes. Ambassador Johnston hadn't been the only high roller involved. That was uncle's headache and he seemed to be enjoying the fuck out of bringing down some of the men and women involved.

Melanie, what can I say? I'd been willing to give her a little break seeing as how she was trying to protect one of her own. I mean I had to ask myself what would I have done if it were my own dad you know? But then that bitch really lost her mind. I guess the specter of her family's shame coupled with whatever had passed between her and my brother had sent her over the edge. That's the only reason I could think of for her going after my girl in front of me.

It had been the Sunday after we'd returned from our honeymoon. Cheeks and I were still in honeymoon mode, but then again when weren't we? We were walking around outside holding hands and making plans. Okay the truth is I'd just fucked her up against a tree out back away from prying eyes. But now we were mellowing out. I still kept her close when I wasn't doing my rounds at the hospital. We spent every free moment together and that's just the way I liked it. She seemed to need that and I'm not one of those dumb fucks who's always talking about needing space. Fuck that, if I could be in her or around her twenty-four seven I'd be on that shit quick.

That day we were reaching the front of the property when this car came speeding up the driveway. Of course my first instinct was to push her behind me and go into fight mode. When the harried looking woman climbed out of the car I barely recognized her at first. Her hair instead of its usual well-coifed do was a ratty mess. Well not exactly but close. She'd lost weight but not in a good way, her clothes were literally hanging on her. I heard the others coming out on the porch behind us but didn't turn.

"The fuck you want?" Okay so I'm not really over her shit. We hadn't seen her in months and my brother never ever brought up her name. In fact he'd forbidden anyone to mention her name to him and we'd all agreed. We'd watched him for the first few months to make sure he was okay but he seemed to be handling his shit. We'd all pretty much moved on and pretended she'd never existed. Her father was under observation in some spa fronting as a nuthouse but I wasn't really interested in that shit. Uncle said he would spend the rest of his life there no matter how cushy it may seem.

Now this bitch was here with her shit. She kept her venomous glare trained on my wife and I felt my hackles rise. If she started blaming her for this shit again I'm gonna lose it. "I repeat what the fuck do you want?" I heard Jules coming down the stairs asking the same thing. His new girl Samantha was here as well probably standing on the porch with the others. I don't know how much of this he'd shared with her but I'm sure she knew some of it. The shit had been the hot topic on the six o'clock news for weeks back when it first broke. I'd shot at plenty an asshole reporter who tried to get onto our property with their bullshit. Uncle had had a time of it keeping me out of jail over that one when I'd clipped one of them in the wing. Ask me if I gave a fuck. I'd had to take her out of school in the end anyway because the fuckers staked out the damn school.

She took a step forward and I checked her move. It was as if she didn't even see me there. She only had eyes for Victoria-Lynn. "This is all your fault you little sniveling bitch. If you'd just stayed with your own kind none of this would've happened. How does it feel to have destroyed innocent people with your lies and filth? Your mother…"

Oh shit; that's as far as she got before a little whirlwind knocked me out of the way and flew at her. It took me half a second to figure out what the fuck had just happened when I saw my wife with her hands wrapped around Melanie's neck. Petra the savage was cheering her the fuck on and I was stuck between two minds. Should I stop her or let her work this shit out of her system? In the end Jules made the decision for me. He pulled me back with a stern "Leave it." What the fuck? I looked from him to the woman whose chest my wife was currently straddling as she tried to make holes in the ground with her head. The woman he'd dated and I believed loved for almost four years.

He must've seen the question and confusion in my eyes. "That bitch wasn't protecting anyone but herself. That whole family are some sick fucks and that's all I'll say on the subject." He turned and walked back up the steps to his new girl. Dad had come down to stand next to me. "You plan on putting an end to this son?" You would think a lot of time had gone by but it couldn't have been more than two minutes. Shit my baby had a busted lip but at least she was kicking ass. I thought it was time to break it up when she started crying and panting. She'd tired herself out whipping that ass. Fucking champ.

"Alright slugger that's enough." I lifted her off her victim who was a bloody crying mess. Damn it must suck to lose at every turn. Dad walked over and bent over Melanie. He's a compassionate sort, me not so much. He finally got her up and out of there. She wasn't screaming out threats anymore. She was just a broken sad mess when she climbed back in her care and drove away. Hopefully that was the last we'd see of her. I took my girl inside and cleaned her up and then let her ride the fuck out of my dick to work off some of that head of steam she still had going on. It was a long night.

Both Crafton men were behind bars. The younger one will never walk again. He was now two cards short of a full deck; drooling on himself and shit last I heard. Serves his ass right, that'll teach him to put his hands on what wasn't his. He's lucky, in some places they chop those shits off. I didn't lose any sleep over that shit either fuck him. Cheeks didn't seem too torn up about it either I guess she finally figured out for herself that he wasn't all there. She'd finally told me all that had happened that day, or I'd dragged it out of her more like. And it took all three men in my family not to do to the hospital and put a bullet in his fucking head.

We pulled through and I let her do everything she needed to do to heal her heart where her mother was concerned. She wanted to know everything about the woman who'd given birth to her so we'd gone digging, and found aunts and uncles who'd been kept away by that fuck. She'd met her family three uncles and an aunt and a set of grandparents who'd never given up hope of seeing her one-day. It was hard for her telling them the truth about what has happened to her mom all those years ago. They too had been told the lie that she'd run off. He'd used his supposed hate for her and what she'd done to him to keep them away from his daughter, the sick twisted fuck. Now she has a relationship with people who love her and more importantly, people who knew her mom and could fill in the gaps so that she was more than just a body dug up in a backyard.

Now we're here this fine summer morning, the birds are chirping outside our bedroom window because their asses are up at the ass crack of dawn and they figure everyone else should be too. I was about to reach for her to give her her morning dose but she rolled out of bed on a run. I was hot on her ass as she knelt over the toilet throwing up her guts. Okay I'm a medical professional so even I couldn't keep pretending that this was anything less than what it was. Fuck. I'd gotten cheeks pregnant. There goes college in the fall. She's gonna kill my ass.

I cleaned her up and sat on the floor with her in my lap until her tummy settled down. "You know what this is right babe?" I held my breath waiting for the tirade. I'll just have to fuck her out of her mad if she went with that. She didn't say anything just took my hand and held it over her tummy. "Yes that's little Stephanie." I pulled her head back so I could see her face and fuck if she wasn't smiling. "You're not mad?"

She turned around in my arms and hugged my neck. "No way. She's our reward. After all the bad things she's our little miracle to make it all better." With my luck she'll be another hardheaded fuck like her mom and the damn dog just another female to run circles around my ass. I stood with her in my arms and headed back to bed. "You feeling okay for this?" She nodded yes and lifted my t-shirt over her head baring her body to me. Her stomach was still flat. There was no sign of pregnancy anywhere. I'll have to make an appointment with the doctor sometime today. Fuck we're gonna have to go half an hour out of town for the nearest female doc. The local gyno is male no way in fuck he was touching her. Fuck that.

THE END

Thanks for reading

You may reach the author @

Jordansilver144@gmail.com

Made in the USA
Middletown, DE
08 March 2022